Frank's attention, however was soon focused on something a lot more dangerous than his captor's bad driving. Pointing at him in the back seat was a .357 Magnun Python, which, according to Colt, was the fastest, most powerful, and best-looking handgun you can own. Frank wasn't about to argue with the quality of their advertising. If the man in the fedora pulled the trigger on that cannon, he'd take out everyone in the line of fire for at least a block.

# MULHOLLAND DRIVE

Also by Robert Hayden

BLACK SUNRISE

Robert Hayden

MULHOLLAND DRIVE

RODEO PRESS
LONDON

For Peter

First published in Great Britain in 2001 by
Rodeo Press, (Publishers) London.

Copyright© Robert Hayden 2001

Quote from *Beneath Mulholland* by David Thomson
is reproduced by permission of the publishers
Little, Brown and Company (UK)

All rights reserved
No part of this book may be reproduced by any means, nor
transmitted, nor translated into machine language without the
permission of the publishers.

Rodeo Press
7 Vicarage Close
Kingswood Surrey KT20 6QF

ISBN 0-9530140-2-9

Typeset in 12pt New Caledonia by
Halcon Printing Ltd., Stonehaven, Scotland.
Printed and bound in England by
Antony Rowe Ltd., Chippenham, Wiltshire.

It is a drive and a highway, running east-west,
the supreme vantage point for the entirety of
Los Angeles and the San Fernando Valley, You can
stand up there and feel like Christ- or the Devil.
Mulholland Drive allows both roles.

David Thomson

PROLOGUE

Tracts of snow still lingered, and here and there through the trees and hills the pale moonlight glinted off the cold black waters of the Hudson as the train followed the river north to Albany. Two hours out of New York the streamlined silver bullet of the 20th Century Limited, 166 tons of stainless steel and polished aluminum, raced silently into the moonlit dark.

On board the black waiter addressed the immaculately attired man on table three who'd just finished dinner. "Will that be all, suh?"

The man looked up, his long fingers caressing the fine crystal glass containing the Remy Martin the waiter had placed in front of him. "It will....Thank you."

The words came out of his mouth like they'd been

carved out of ice. The man spoke in perfect English, but with a clipped hard edge he could not entirely dispel. His face was expressionless, but had just the right amount of good looks to make you think he might be somebody. Coldest of all were the eyes, a chilling, pale gun-metal. If the eyes were the window to the soul, thought the waiter, then this guy was damn near frozen.

He straightened an ashtray and nervously brushed some imaginary crumbs off the table. Some kind of foreigner, he decided as he left, wondering vaguely what nationality the man might be. Probably one of those European movie directors he'd heard so much about, they were reputed to be a chilly lot. The waiter was usually very good at placing people, but this time he was fairly wide of the mark.

The Hudson J-Class locomotive had left Grand Central at six that evening for the 961 mile journey to Chicago via Albany, Rochester and Buffalo. The twelve car Pullman streamliner was the pride of the New York Central Railroad. From the moment the passengers boarded from the 260 yard maroon carpet at the terminal, their every whim was catered for.

By now the dining car had begun to get extremely busy. There were, of course, the usual quota of movie stars on board. The waiter had recognised Katharine Hepburn back at Grand Central, but so far she had not appeared for dinner.

If the man at table three was impressed by any of this he did not show it. He picked up his cognac, swirled it around the glass and glanced absently through the slatted venetian blinds. Rows of lights flashed past the windows like tracers as they sped through some small upstate town. Just as suddenly darkness returned to mirror the windows once more.

Sometime later, the man traveling under the name of Alexander March finished off his cognac, rose to his feet, and returned to the privacy of his suite. Carefully locking the door he retrieved a brown leather traveling bag from the rack. He snapped open the catch, removed a book, a pack of cigarettes and his night attire. For a second his fingers brushed the cool steel surface of the 9mm Walther. His lips drew back in a cold mirthless smile as he changed and, after reading for a short time, he finally settled in his berth to sleep.

Only one thought engaged him as he closed his eyes. He was imagining the look of surprise and horror on the face of his old colleague when they met. It would undoubtedly be his last.

He was awoken next morning by the rattling and clicking of the points as the train made its way slowly into Chicago. By noon, with the through cars attached to the Santa Fe Super Chief, they'd be ready for the remaining thirty-seven hour run to the movie capital of the world.

Hollywood.

LOS ANGELES, 1939

1

Tony Senna had pulled the Chevy into the curb just far enough away from the house so that he could get a good view, but not close enough to be suspicious. It had been a while since he'd done a stake-out on his own like this, but one thing he had learned; no two of them went down the same.

Claymont Drive, a ribbon of smooth concrete, wound on for another couple of dusty miles before petering out in the scrubby green hills near the reservoir. One of the countless roads springing up on the acres of new sub-divison around the city.

Up ahead the road was empty for as far as he could see. He'd been watching for at least an hour and his eyes were beginning to tire. He stretched his arms, tipped back the pearl-gray fedora on his head and took a deep draw on his cigarette. The radio played a Tommy Dorsey number very softly. Humming the tune quietly to himself, he checked the binoculars again for focus. He might need to use them quick.

A block west on Cahuenga the murmur of traffic had gradually faded with the lateness of the hour. Only an occasional sound betrayed its presence. To the east a pale glow rose from the city merging into the black canopy above. The stars glittered like hard bright diamonds on a velvet tray.

Six twenty-one was about a third of a block along, on the crest of a slight rise, with only a few low shrubs out front surrounding a parched lawn. Stake-outs had never been one of his favorite tasks, especially on Saturday nights. If he hadn't had this tip-off from Benny, he'd be sitting in the Delmar Club with Frank and a couple of broads right now, celebrating his good day at the track. Frank would probably have a go at him for taking the Friday off, but what the hell. He was more than making up for it out here.

The house itself was not quite what he'd expected, but the number was right so it had to be the one. Long, low, ranch style Spanish, with a barrel tile roof, stucco walls and an arched front porch, it seemed a little too opulent for a bank clerk, but then people were always full of surprises. The windows had wrought-iron grilles set in the stonework, but no lights showed from them or any other part of the house he could see.

Next to him on the right hand side of the street was

a vacant lot, thick with pepper trees and oaks fresh with leaves from the winter rains. Occasionally a soft wind rustled through them.

He waited. An hour crawled by.

He checked the luminous dial of his watch. Ten-seventeen. It was a long wait, but it could be the final piece of evidence he needed to wrap this case up. Most were pretty straightforward, this one didn't look like being any different. A Leica with an F-2 lens and flash attachment lay on the seat beside him, ready for any eventuality.

He rolled down the window. The night air was sharp and chill. He took one final drag on the cigarette, flicked it out in a glowing arc and watched it die slowly on the smooth concrete.

Turning the radio a little lower, he took a slug from his hip flask, and settled back a little more comfortably in his seat. After a minute his eyes began to close. Were there any cases out there other than marital infidelity and locating the missing wives of store salesmen? He could only hope.

It was just after eleven when headlights flashed in the rearview mirror and he heard a car go by. He jerked awake and hurriedly groped for the binoculars on the seat. It was a little darker now, the sky was overcast and the stars had gone. He adjusted the focus slightly. There was enough light to see a gleaming black coupe swing onto the driveway of the house and roll to a halt.

Immediately the lights snapped off and the motor cut.

A frown creased his forehead. This wasn't the car he was expecting to see, it looked big enough to be a Cadillac. For a moment nothing happened. Then two dark figures emerged, hats pulled well down, and hurried along the short paved walk to the house.

"What the hell?" Tony whispered under his breath. "What happened to the broad?"

A slight shiver went down his back. Something didn't add up: there should have been a woman there. "Who are these guys?" he mouthed silently, leaning forward to get a better view. The binoculars caught the brief flash of a face in the strip of light from the doorway.

Something went clicking quietly through his brain. An image he couldn't quite recall. A face he was sure he recognised. From where, from when? One thing was certain: these weren't the people he had been following for the better part of a week.

A slight sound outside the car raised the hairs on back of his neck. How could that be? Unless someone had dropped off back down the street. He hadn't heard another car. He quickly checked the rearview mirror but saw nothing. Sensing danger he turned around to look. The vacant lot, perhaps they'd come....

Tony Senna never heard the vicious flat zip of the silenced slug as it dissolved the rear quarter-light in a hail of shattered glass and drilled neatly through his right temple splattering the driver's window with a mixture of blood, gore and bone.

In that last millisecond of life, as the slug tore its way through his brain, he remembered the face he'd seen. He tried desperately to say it, but no sound came from his mouth, and there was no-one there to listen. His lifeless body jerked involuntarily then slumped sideways across the seat, blood pooling on the leatherette, eyes vacant, staring sightlessly upward.

Printed on his retina for eternity would be that one final indelible image.

2

Harry's Cocktail Lounge on Sunset never had any real claim to fame. Well, at least not since '37 when they found some lush with his throat cut jammed in a garbage bin in the alley out back. That did get them on the front page of the *Los Angeles Examiner.* It didn't exactly get them any new business though, far from it, and they never did find the killer.

It was, however, situated almost exactly halfway between Frank DeMarco's business address and his one-bedroom apartment on Kenmore, which suited him down to the ground. Hence, when Lieutenant Phil Brady of Homicide Division wanted to find him anytime after six, he knew at least where to start looking.

Frank sat on one of the chrome-legged stools at the

end of the bar, staring morosely into his drink. A week had gone by since they'd found his partner's body stuffed in the trunk of his car out on Mulholland. So far his enquiries had led him precisely nowhere.

Tony never talked much about his cases; matrimonial work was not usually filled with murder and mayhem. This case had not appeared to be an exception. Frank had carefully gone through what paperwork there was. Nothing there looked like providing even the remotest of leads. He was also certain that if Tony had had any serious enemies, he'd have known about them.

The bartender, a big man with glossy black hair and a dead-pan expression, was studiously polishing highball glasses midway down the bar when Frank pushed his empty glass forward.

"Same again, Joe," he muttered.

The bartender put down the glass, threw the towel over his shoulder and moved toward Frank. "This ain't gonna bring Tony back," he said, putting his big hands on the bar.

"I'm well aware of that," replied Frank tonelessly.

The bartender shrugged, reached back, produced a bottle of Hiram Walker and refilled the glass. "On the tab?" he said.

"On the tab. And this time leave the bottle."

The bartender showed no emotion as he moved away. He'd seen and dealt with enough customers to knew when people wanted to be left alone.

Frank splashed some seltzer from the syphon into

the glass and proceeded to drink. A few more of the regular crowd had begun to drift into the bar and the hum of conversation had risen to more like its normal level. Frank was soon aware of someone sliding onto the red, leather-topped stool next to him.

"Hullo, Frank, I thought I'd find you here," said Brady quietly.

"Yeah, well, you found me. So what?"

"That's no way to greet an old friend."

"A friend? While you guys downtown are busy trying to hang this rap on me?".

Brady laid his brown fedora carefully on the bar. "Frank, you know that's not what I think, and you know I don't run the department."

"I guess that makes it alright." Frank sank the remainder of his bourbon.

Brady sighed. "I didn't say it was alright, just that's how it is. We ran down the couple in the case Tony was working on. Both are in the clear. You sure there's nothing more you can tell us?"

"I told you already. Some guy thought his wife was cheating on him. Tony was on the case. That's it. Just routine."

Brady lapsed into silence. The bartender, sensing a break in the conversation, stopped his monotonous task and moved along the counter. "Drink, Lieutenant?"

"Gimme a beer."

Brady lit a cigarette while he was waiting. He dropped the match into an ashtray, watched it curl and blacken, and waited some more till the bartender slid a tall cold glass across the bar. He sipped a little before turning back to Frank.

"You've got to admit this is a professional looking job, and the way the Captain sees it, the guy nearest to him is the first suspect. Added to which you don't have much of an alibi."

"Alibi? What the hell do I need an alibi for? You think I'm gonna kill my partner for taking the odd day out at the race track? That's the only thing we had any disagreement about in the last couple of months."

"Hell, no." Brady's voice trailed off. "You should know by now how Malone thinks, Frank. It just looks bad that's all." He sipped his beer. "He's expecting me to bring you in for further questioning."

"That bastard."

"Look, I dislike Malone just as much as you do, but he's just doing his job."

"Yeah, well, he can do it without me."

"Okay, Frank, let's forget it. It's a bad idea." Brady took a long pull at his beer. "Maybe you can tell *me* something. Didn't Benny Walsh used to hang around with Tony a lot?"

"He did."

"Any idea where I can find him?"

"Gone up to 'Frisco I think."

"Permanently?"

"No, he went to visit his sister as far as I know. Don't worry, I'll let you know when he gets back."

They both sat for a while in silence, drinking and staring across the bar. Frank knew that Brady was one of those few and far between things in the LAPD, an honest cop, and *he* was just doing *his* job, but it irked him all the same.

"You know what really puzzles me?" said Brady eventually.

"No. Surprise me."

"What the hell was Tony doing out on a god-forsaken spot like Mulholland when the case he was working on was in West Hollywood? That's a clear five miles away."

"Answering questions like that, Phil, is one of the reasons the city pays you every month and gives you a pension."

"Yeah, well," grumbled Brady. "Who'd have a lousy road like that named after him anyway."

"Don't you know anything, Phil? Mulholland was superintendent of the Water Department back in the twenties. He brought the water to L.A. If it hadn't been for him, you'd be out of a job; round here'd be nothing but dry scrub."

"How do you know that, Frank?"

"There was a case a couple of years back. Some people buying up water rights in the valley. Most of the story came out then. Don't you ever read the papers, Phil?"

"Naw, just makes me worry about things I haven't got time to worry about. Anyway for what it's worth, we're not sure that's where Tony was killed."

"How do you figure?"

"He was shot in the car, blood on the passenger seat showed that. Then the body was moved into the trunk. That we do know. But there were no other traces at the scene, so maybe it was done someplace else, then moved out to Mulholland."

"Meaning, if we find out where, we might find out why."

"I guess."

"Did you find the slug?"

"Lodged down by the gas pedal, pretty well mashed up, but looked like a .38."

"No other angles?"

"None. And still no sign of any relatives. You'd have thought someone would have come forward by now. It made all the front pages."

Frank was silent. People came and went in the bar, but no one approached them, as if they sensed something was taking place they'd rather not be involved in.

"Any idea where Tony came from originally?" asked Brady, draining the last of his beer.

Frank shook his head. "None at all. The only place I ever recall him mentioning was Chicago. He'd done some private eye work up there once, but he never talked about it and never said where he grew up either."

"Chicago." Brady sat up. "You think he could have been in some sort of trouble up there?"

"No reason to think so," said Frank. "If there was, he

never mentioned it."

"How long ago was this?"

"Couple of years give or take."

Brady pushed his empty glass away and sat for a moment in thought. "Some of those guys up there got awful long memories, Frank. Could be they just found him."

"Could be," said Frank slowly. "Could be." He stubbed out his cigarette on the chrome ashtray on the bar. "I've a hunch it's a whole lot closer to home than that."

3

Frank DeMarco's office was a suite of rooms on the third floor of the Farrel building on Sunset, a couple of blocks west of NBC's recently completed Radio City. A streamlined, curving, Moderne affair that took up most of the block. Frank's office building had no such pretensions, but it served his purpose just the same.

Tall, slim, and solidly built Frank weighed about one eighty. His black hair was brushed straight back. He wore a well cut dark gray suit, a white shirt and a blue silk tie. A few years back he'd been chief investigator for the DA's office. But that was another story.

Frank picked up a newspaper, crossed the lobby and joined a couple waiting for the elevator. They were gazing intently at each other as if the rest of the world didn't exist. Frank wondered which one of the offices upstairs they were headed for; he hoped it wasn't his. When the doors opened, the couple got in and Frank followed. The operator gave everyone a bored glance, moved the handle and took the car up. Frank got out on three. The couple were still gazing into each other's eyes, he wondered how long it would be before they were eyeing each other's throats.

There were several doorways down the wide hallway housing an assortment of businesses, lawyers being the most prevalent, followed closely by accountants and the odd dentist. Frank paused at Suite 324: the frosted glass door panel read DeMarco and Senna Investigations. The solid black letters loomed larger than usual. He didn't want to think about it right now, but sooner or later he'd have to get around to removing Tony's name.

Ellie, his secretary, was typing diligently when he entered. "Hi, boss," she smiled wanly. "Any news?"

"No, angel. Nothing yet. Sorry."

"Here's a note of your calls," she said brightening up a little. She tore the top sheet off her pad. Frank went through an inner glass-panelled door to his office.

The room had a singularly spare look; a desk, a bureau, a couple of filing cabinets and a water cooler. Sunshine streamed through the slatted blinds casting angled shadows across the worn leatherette divan underneath the window. Frank dropped into the wooden swivel chair behind the desk, lit up a cigarette and scanned the list.

Somebody wanted him to find a missing girl-friend, another a partner who'd skipped out with most of the cash from the business. The third was an insurance scam. Nothing, he decided, that couldn't wait till later. He had his feet on the desk reading the *Examiner* when Ellie came in with some coffee.

"Thanks, sweetheart," he said.

He watched her as she went out. Ellie was a sweet kid with a good figure. Not one you'd crawl over broken glass to get to; more like someone you'd take home and introduce to the folks.

Frank was between cases, so he'd spent the last week trying to get a lead on Tony's murder. The truth, of course, was that he hadn't been able to concentrate on anything else. However, the result so far had been a very large zero. Even the news-boys were finding it hard to come up with anything new. The story had now been dropped from the headlines to an inside page; STILL NO CLUES IN MULHOLLAND KILLING it said.

There was one slim hope however, as he had told Brady. Benny was due back later this week and might just might be able to give them a lead.

Benny was an oddball sort of a guy. Most thought he was a little punchy, although he'd been a fair welter in his time. Anyway he'd attached himself to the place as a sort of gofer. He'd hang around the bar the cops used and pick up all sorts of information. Apart from that he was pretty good at tailing people; no-one ever gave him a second glance. Frank slipped him a few bucks now and again which kept him in beer money.

He knew Benny had been helping Tony out that last week before going up to Frisco to visit his sister. Some guy she'd been living with had put her in hospital.

Frank was sipping his coffee and contemplating further when the phone rang.

"Ellie," he yelled. "Can you get that?"

There was no reply. Damn, he thought, she must have slipped out to the girls' room. He picked up the phone.

"Hello?"

"Is this DeMarco and Senna Investigations?"

"Yes, Frank DeMarco speaking."

The brisk secretarial voice continued. "Hold on, please. I have a call for you."

Frank's mind conjured up an immediate image.

"Mr DeMarco?" This was a new voice, heavy, foreign, guttural. It continued. "My name is Ullrich, Karl Ullrich. Perhaps you've heard of me? I'm a movie producer."

"Uhh..." replied Frank, racking his brains to see if he could remember any such person. He couldn't. "What can I do for you, Mr Ullrich?"

"You are the private detective - yes?"

"We are." He realised the 'we' part of that statement wasn't quite true, but he was disinclined at the moment to get into lengthy explanations about it. "How can I help you?" he said finally.

"I should like very much to meet you and talk about

that. Can you make the Brown Derby for lunch today? It's on Vine half a block south of Hollywood Boulevard. Then I am better able to explain."

Frank, who was perfectly well aware of where the Brown Derby was, mused for a moment.

"Well now, let's see if I am free." He ran his finger down the empty page of his diary. "Yes, I think that will be alright." It wasn't every day he was invited to a free lunch. Added to which, right now, he didn't have anything better to do.

"Splendid," replied Ullrich. "Would twelve-thirty suit you?"

"Fine. How will I recognise you?"

"Just ask for my table. The waiter will show you."

"Okay," replied Frank.

He put the telephone back in its cradle thoughtfully. Ullrich, Ullrich, never heard of him. But that didn't mean much; movie people were appearing out of the woodwork these days.

Ellie stuck her head round the door. She'd heard Frank hang up the phone.

"Sorry, boss, I had to go to the....."

"The can, yeah, I guessed. Can you nip down to the lobby and see if you can get a copy of the *Hollywood Reporter*?"

"Sure," said Ellie, raising her eyebrows. "You thinking of going into the movies?"

"Scram," he said. She was out the door before he could find anything suitable to throw.

Ellie duly returned with a copy of the *Reporter*. Frank spent the next twenty minutes reading the latest movie news. He found what he was looking for on the next to last page. The third item in a gossip column.

"Warner Brothers Producer Karl Ullrich
is now well ahead with his new movie.
Rumor has it Edward G Robinson
is playing the lead. Word on the street is
it's likely to be highly controversial.
So far no one is talking, but watch
this space."

Frank leaned back in his chair. Now what would some big-time movie producer want his services for? Perhaps his wife had run off with Sam Goldwyn.

The Brown Derby on Vine Street, built in the Spanish mission style and probably the most famous restaurant in the world, buzzed with the usual crowd from the movie colony. Writers, directors, producers, agents and stars et al. Although, at any given moment, you could bet that fifty percent of the clientele were watching the other fifty percent. Frank recognised one or two famous faces, but couldn't quite put names to them.

"Can I help you?" purred the head waiter as Frank entered the foyer.

"Yeah," Frank said. "Mr Ullrich's table please."

Immediately the waiter became deferential.

"Certainly, sir. Would you follow me, please?"

The interior was something to behold. The dining room consisted of an interlocking arrangement of low booths upholstered in brown leather. The walls were hung with dozens of caricatures of the stars.

Frank spotted a stoutish figure in a booth on his own as they crossed the room. This looked like his man. The waiter stood aside as they arrived.

"Ah, Mr DeMarco, I presume. Please sit down," said Ullrich waving his hand expansively. "Would you care for a drink?"

Another waiter in a starched white linen jacket had appeared. Frank slid into the booth. Ullrich was already halfway through what looked like a bourbon.

"A Manhattan, please." said Frank.

The waiter melted away.

"Thank you for coming at such short notice, Mr DeMarco," Ullrich beamed.

He was everything Frank had expected including the expensive suit, the flashy bow-tie and the fat brown cigar. He had straight black hair, heavy eyebrows and a neatly trimmed moustache and beard. His body, in its early forties, looked the victim of too many long lunches.

Frank's drink arrived. The waiter must be trying to impress him. Or somebody. Or maybe he just wanted to get into the movies. Frank figured the second option was the more likely, given who he was sitting with. After some consultation they ordered. That ought to get rid of the waiter for at least fifteen minutes.

He sipped the Manhattan appreciatively. They certainly knew how to mix a drink.

"Now, Mr DeMarco, can you tell me something about yourself?"

"Well, Mr Ullrich, there isn't really a whole lot to tell. I'm a licensed private investigator. I've been in business for a couple of years and until last week I had a partner. I drink a little, play seven card stud, take a lady out once in a while and most times carry a gun. What I don't do is handle divorce cases. My partner used to, but unfortunately he's no longer around."

Ullrich's brows came together. He looked a little concerned.

"I hesitate to ask, Mr DeMarco. Did something happen to him?"

"It did, in spades. Somebody shot him last week."

"Shot.....Good heavens. Is he....?"

"I'm afraid so Mr Ullrich. I'm afraid so."

Ullrich took a large gulp from his glass and promptly signalled for another.

"Does that mean you're not available?"

"No, it doesn't, Mr Ullrich. Like they say in the movies, life goes on. By the way, how did you happen to pick me? The LA directory's full of P.I's."

"Ah, you'll have to ask my secretary, Miss Cain, that question, I just told her to get the best man available." A second bourbon had appeared in front of Ullrich and he grabbed it with both hands. A smile slowly reappeared on his face as he took a long drink.

"Perhaps now we can get down to business?"

Frank sat back and sipped again at his Manhattan. "Well, you can start by telling me what this is all about, Mr Ullrich?"

Ullrich leaned forward conspiritorially. "I need to hire a bodyguard," he said softly, glancing around the room. Although, with the level of noise in this place, he needn't have bothered.

Frank observed him coolly. "That's not exactly in my line of work either."

"You don't understand, Mr DeMarco," Ullrich said in an urgent tone. "I have received some threatening letters."

Frank slid the Manhattan around his mouth. "Any idea who they might be from?"

"That's what I was rather hoping you'd be able to find out."

"It wasn't meant to be a specific question, Mr Ullrich. You must have some idea surely?"

"I assure you, Mr DeMarco none whatever."

Either Ullrich was playing his cards close to his chest or he really had no idea who was threatening him. Frank wasn't sure which. "Have you talked to the cops about this?"

"Never. I can't afford that kind of publicity. I'd be the laughing stock of the town. This must be handled very quietly."

Frank set his drink down carefully "You have these letters?"

"Well, not with me."

"Very well, Mr Ullrich, We need to talk further. Can I come to your office tomorrow?"

"Certainly, certainly. Say about 11am?" He scribbled his signature on the back of a studio pass he produced from his top pocket. "Just hand this to the gateman. They'll let you through."

Just then the waiter reappeared with the food. This guy really was fast. They ought to think about entering him in the Kentucky Derby.

It was on the way back to the office that Frank noticed the tail.

4

Mulholland Drive tracks westward for fifty long and frequently dusty miles along the ridges of the Santa Monica mountains on its twisting journey to the ocean. A road starting nowhere and going nowhere. A memorial to a man most people neither knew nor cared about.

Tony's car had been found just a few hundred yards from the intersection with Hillpark, on a lonely stretch of blacktop where the road wound back down to meet its starting point on Cahuenga.

The morning air was crisp and clear at this elevation, with a stiff breeze, as Brady spent several minutes re-examining the scene. Even the few tracks there had been had now vanished in the bone dry dust of the roadside. There wasn't one speck of real evidence to show that anything had happened here at all. He stood for a moment shaking his head absently and looking at the view, the wind against his face. From here you could see across Hollywood, Beverley Hills and all the way down to Bay City. Then nothing but the flat metallic-blue mass of the Pacific, rolling on to the end of the world.

It was sometime after eleven that morning when Brady got back to homicide. He'd gone on to re-check the statements of the couple involved in Senna's last case, but nothing new had emerged there either. Both husband and wife had stuck to their original stories. He knew perfectly well the wife was lying, but there wasn't a whole lot he could do about it.

His next port of call had been the LA County morgue, never one of his favourite destinations. Tony's body was still on ice and would be until the case was solved. At least they didn't have to contend with grieving relatives. So far, as he had mentioned to Frank, they'd not been able to trace a single soul. But Frank had mentioned Chicago, so he'd sent the CPD a full report. There was always a chance they might come up with something.

He grabbed a coffee from the pot in the squad room and went through to his office. A few moments later the burly figure of Sergeant Gus Harrigan appeared in the doorway.

"Good morning, Lieutenant."

"That depends on what you're here for."

Harrigan looked slightly uncomfortable. "Captain said to see him as soon as you came in."

"Right.....I thought as much," said Brady rummaging in his tray. "You got the Senna file?"

"I....er...think the Captain took it."

Brady didn't blink an eyelid, but gulped some coffee and headed off down the marble-floored corridor. He didn't need to be clairvoyant to know what this was all about.

Captain Malone, Chief of Detectives, was a thick-necked bull of a man and not at all easy to like. Brady had taken all of fifteen minutes at their first meeting to try. That's how long it was before he realised people like Malone didn't really want to be liked. His type ruled partly by fear and partly by intimidation. He enjoyed rubbing people up the wrong way just see their reaction.

Malone liked his cases tied up in neat bundles and filed under solved. That was the way you got ahead in the department. What the hell if a few innocent guys got creamed, that's the system - right? We don't make the laws, he was fond of saying, we just carry them out.

Brady pushed through the outer gate where a couple of secretaries were typing with some vigor. One looked up and nodded him through.

Brady noticed the Senna file front and centre on the desk as he knocked and went in. There were two chairs in front of the desk. He waited for the Captain to look up before assuming he'd be there long enough to sit in one.

"Sit down, Phil," said Malone.

So far so good, thought Brady, sitting down carefully.

Malone continued, "I was expecting to see Frank DeMarco in here this morning." His voice had just the right amount of acid in it.

Brady sat down and kept his face expressionless. "I talked to DeMarco at some length last night Captain, and I don't think he knows any more than he's already told us."

Malone's ruddy face was hard and impassive. His tone didn't change. "What makes you think that, Phil?"

"It just doesn't figure. What possible reason could he have for killing his partner? Why would he do that? It's just too obvious a move. There's nothing particular between them, no motive. They handled different sides of the business, so there wasn't any conflict of interest. And besides, he was having drinks with some broad at the Delmar Club on Sunset all evening, and didn't leave until 1am."

Malone leaned back in his chair, and put his thumbs in his braces.

"You check that out?"

"As far as possible, yes."

Malone's eyes were like flint. He leaned forward across the desk and flicked open the file. "According to this Senna was killed around midnight. You know as well as I do, Phil, there's so much going on at that fucking joint anybody could duck in and out of there anytime with nobody the wiser. Exactly the sort of alibi you would expect DeMarco to have."

Brady was silent for a moment. He knew what he said next would be critical. "Look, Captain, there's no hard evidence to tie this killing to DeMarco. There are just too many things that don't add up. Where the body was dumped for one, and the fact that there had to be two people involved in getting him there. Dead men don't drive cars. We're trying to get a sighting of the car anywhere near the scene between ten and midnight. If we can find out where he was killed, we might find out why. We just need some more time."

Malone's face was as hard as ever, but Brady sensed he'd won the point.

"What about this guy Benny Walsh. Where does he fit in to the picture?"

"Benny's just a gofer," said Brady. "Used to be in the fight game, hung around with Senna a lot and bummed around generally. Anyway he's out of it, took off to 'Frisco to see his sister on the Friday. Still there as far as we know, but we'll talk to him when he gets back. Maybe he can wise us up with some details on the case Senna was working on. But I don't expect much."

Malone picked up a cigar from the box on his desk, ran it under his nose then jabbed his stubby finger at the page. "I see here you've got an enquiry in to the Chicago PD. What's that all about?"

"According to DeMarco, Senna worked up there as a PI for a time. I'm also trying to get a line on any relatives and…er…anything else that might be of interest."

"What exactly do you mean anything else?"

"Well, there could be a connection with an old case, it has all the hallmarks of a contract job."

Malone fixed his eyes on Brady.

"Okay, Phil," he said slowly. "I'll go with you on this one. I guess DeMarco's not going anywhere. You got until the end of the week." He slid the file back across the desk and looked up at Brady before he removed his hand. "Don't screw up. And... let me know the minute you get anything."

Brady rose and picked up the file. He could feel Malone's stare on his back as he left the room.

5

Frank DeMarco checked his mirror one more time, made a left onto Cahuenga Boulevard and headed north. He had a hunch he was being followed, but so far he hadn't managed to spot anybody.

There was an outside chance he'd been wrong about the tail yesterday, but somehow he didn't think so. It always paid to be careful. Too late now to remind Tony of that, but Frank wasn't aiming to go out of business just yet. He had no idea who the killer might have been. Maybe someone from Tony's past really had caught up with him, but, somehow, he didn't think so. This felt like something else. There were all sorts out there, you learnt that very fast in this business.

Either way you could be just as dead.

It was a bright February morning and the chill air

was fresh and clean. Off to his right the snow covered peaks of the distant San Gabriel mountains, behind the city, glinted in the early sun. He turned onto Barham Boulevard. In the distance he could see the water tower of Universal Studios. It was about here that the City of Los Angeles ended and Burbank began.

Right now he'd other things on his mind. So far in his brief career he'd managed to avoid contact with the inhabitants of the movie world. You could walk the boulevards day after day for a long time and never see a star. Of course if you knew their habitats, like any other big game, they weren't all that difficult to find. It was just that for the most part the studios took care of their own dirty laundry.

Frank had gotten Ellie to work yesterday, movie fan that he knew she was, running down everything there was to know about friend Ullrich, right down to his size in argyle socks. So far most of what she had uncovered was straightforward enough.

Karl Ullrich had arrived on the Hollywood scene a year ago from New York. Made a couple of pictures and scored a modest hit on his last movie "Shades of Gray," a courtroom drama. Frank had some vague recollection of having seen it, but he couldn't recall much about it.

Ullrich had since negotiated an independent deal with First National for his present picture, the subject of which was, for the moment, under wraps. There wasn't much about his personal life other than the usual about-town gossip, but Ellie was still digging. If someone was threatening Ullrich there had to be some damn good reason.

Warner Bros and First National's main entrance was at Hollywood Way and Olive. Frank turned the black LaSalle roadster up to the gate and pulled up. A big burly uniformed security guard appeared from the gatehouse.

"Yes, sir?"

Frank produced the pass.

"Oh.. right, sir. Just take the next left, you can park anywhere in front of the building."

The barrier rose.

The front office was a two story white stucco affair with a overhanging red tile roof, standard California style. Out front a row of palms down the center aisle of the car park afforded some shade. Frank pulled in between a red Cord roadster and a cream Cadillac. The car park looked like a set-up for a glossy magazine spread of the latest models. He was beginning to feel inferior already.

He pushed through the swing doors and checked the directory on the wall. Ullrich's name had a line all to itself. The executive offices were on the second floor. So far so good. What he came upon next was probably going to change his life forever.

Behind a chrome-edged black desk in the reception area was a vision wearing a hounds-tooth business suit over a white sheer silk top. She gave him a glance that would have melted the polar ice-cap. A soft mane of blonde hair, full of gleams and glints, surrounded an oval face with skin the color of honey and eyes as blue as a California morning. Her softly-curving lips were the color of cherries.

Her other curves were in all the right places.

"Miss Cain?" he asked, hoping his voice didn't give away the thought that had just entered his head.

"You must be Frank DeMarco," she replied evenly.

"How. . . ?"

She smiled a little smile and glanced down. "That's what it says here on my pad, Mr DeMarco, and they are pretty careful who they let in at the gate. Take a seat, there's someone with Mr Ullrich, but I'm sure he won't be more than a moment."

Frank held her gaze for a second. She had that rare quality of class and breeding you know the instant you see it, but are unable somehow to define. He sat in one of the big comfortable armchairs ranged along the wall. Above them hung a number of studio publicity shots in glossy black frames. He recognised Bogart, Cagney, and Raft. He was glancing idly through a copy of *Photoplay* when he heard raised voices from behind the doors of the office. They appeared to be somewhat heated.

"You can't take out those lines," shouted a voice. "It sets up a situation that develops later. They gotta stay in."

"I don't give a damn. I don't like them, take them out."

"You can't take them out without a good reason."

"The hell I can't. I'm the producer and I'm running this movie."

The door crashed open.

"Well, screw you and the movie." A slightly flushed figure in shirt sleeves slammed the door and stormed off into the corridor.

Miss Cain appeared completely unfazed. She stopped typing, reached out a manicured hand, and spoke for a moment into the intercom. "You can go right in, Mr DeMarco."

Frank, who had also watched the scene without a flicker of emotion, rose, and walked through the double doors to the inner sanctum. It certainly lived up to all he had imagined a Hollywood producer's office to be. Not that he could recollect any particular occasion when such a thought might have occupied his mind.

The room, lined with dark wood paneling, had several built-in bookshelves and a glass display case holding numerous awards. Ullrich, cigar in mouth, rose from behind a vast desk which was only slightly smaller than the deck of an aircraft carrier. If his previous visitor had upset him, he showed no outward sign of it. They exchanged the usual pleasantries before getting down to business. Ullrich singled out a small key from bunch in his pocket, unlocked a lower drawer and produced a large manilla envelope. He slipped out two folded sheets of paper and slid them across the desk. They were made up of cut-out capital letters arranged and stuck down.

FOR HE WHO LIVES MORE LIVES
THAN ONE,
MORE DEATHS THAN ONE MUST DIE.

The second read:

NOTHING IN YOUR LIFE BECOMES YOU
LIKE LEAVING IT.

Frank examined them carefully. Someone had obviously laboured long and hard one quiet winter evening, but they gave him no clues. He slipped them back into the envelope and looked across at Ullrich. "The usual thing, cut from magazines, impossible to trace. When did these arrive?"

"The first about three weeks back, the other last week."

"Are you sure this isn't some sort of practical joke?"

"I have considered that, Mr DeMarco, but I'm sure someone would have owned up to it by now. Since no-one has, I can only assume they're serious."

"Rather oddly worded, wouldn't you say?"

"They're probably quotations. From where, I confess I don't know. Whether that has any particular significance..." his voice trailed off.

"Maybe yes, maybe no," finished Frank. "It certainly

seems as if our friend likes to play games. It is possible, of course, that's just all it is. The real question, though, is how long does he intend the game to go on for, and what does he intend to do when it ends?"

Ullrich's face looked a trifle paler. "That is the part that worries me."

"Another question," said Frank. "I know you said you didn't want to bring the cops into this, but you seem to have some pretty heavy security around here. What do you need me for?"

"You mean those guys who wander around in uniform and guard the stages and the gates?" Ullrich threw up his hands in horror. "You got to be kidding. Those guys couldn't find their way out of a movie theater unless the lights were up. The real question, Mr DeMarco, is do you think you can find this person?"

"Finding people is what I do best, Mr Ullrich, even those who don't want to be found. However, unless you propose to start wearing a suit of armor, there's not a whole lot I can do about you personally. Your best bet will be to keep with as many people as possible, and avoid going out in public unless it is absolutely necessary."

"Very well," replied Ullrich resignedly. "That is going to be difficult, but I'll try. Does that mean you'll take the job?"

"Well, I guess I've come this far."

"Splendid, splendid. By the way we haven't discussed your fee?"

"Twenty-five dollars a day plus expenses."

"You will forgive me for smiling a little, Mr DeMarco, but some people in this business get that an hour. Anyway I'll make it thirty a day, plus a bonus of $250 dollars when you find out who is responsible."

"That's more than generous, Mr Ullrich. But let's not get too hasty, we have one small problem. Since the culprit is more than likely an employee, I can't just go strolling around here without some reason. No point in frightening our man off for him to return another day."

"Hmm...no, I see your point. In that case we'll have to find you a job on my new picture. Wait, I've got it, we'll make you a story consultant. We'll even give you an office. How's that?"

"But what exactly would I do?"

"Nothing. Anything. Doesn't matter. Believe me, Mr DeMarco, there are people here on the payroll who have been doing exactly that and getting away with it for years." He laughed heartily. "But if that worries you, we can inundate you with enough paperwork to fool Jack Warner himself."

He glanced at his watch. "Look I've got a lunch meeting with my director. I'm going to get Lois, my secretary, to take you to lunch at the commissary. We'll talk again later. She's the only one, incidentally, who knows anything about the notes. I had her type some copies for you to take away."

Ullrich put the envelope back into the drawer, then tipped the key on his internal speaker. "Lois, can you come in a moment?"

Frank wondered if all this was for real, it felt like he'd walked into the middle of a movie. Lois came in and leaned casually against the door jamb. It was his first chance to see her full figure. Taller than average, five eight at a guess, with the sort of body you usually see in your dreams, the only difference was in this scene she had her clothes *on*.

6

Ellie dropped the copy of *Modern Screen* where she'd been reading a review of Bogart's latest movie, *King of the Underworld*, and picked up the phone at the second ring.

"Senna and DeMarco Inves...."

"Yeah, it's me, Ellie."

"Boss, I thought you would be back hours ago?"

"I got a little detained."

Ellie pouted.

"Was she that good?"

"Now, now, Ellie. I'll pretend I didn't hear that. Anyone call?"

"No calls, but Benny's back. He was really broken up when I told him about Tony, it was the first he'd heard. You know he never reads anything but the *Daily Racing*

Form. Not that it would have made the 'Frisco dailies anyway."

"Where is he now?" asked Frank.

"Said he was going out to get a beer, and would be back shortly."

"Okay. When he comes in, tell him to wait. I'll be there as soon as I can."

Frank hung up the phone and rose from his perch on the edge of Lois's desk. He might have guessed Benny would take Tony's death pretty hard. Like walking into a right cross.

"Thanks. I guess I'd better take off," he said looking at Lois. "Some loose ends to take care of."

She looked back with those big blue eyes. "I'll call you tomorrow, as soon as Mr Ullrich comes in."

Frank nodded, lit up a cigarette and blew some smoke in the air. "Take care," was all he said.

He was in a thoughtful mood as he headed out to the car park. It was too early to start making any assumptions vis-a-vis Ullrich, but when people started sending threatening letters there was usually a dame involved in the equation somewhere. That or money. Follow the money was an old maxim, although he couldn't quite see where that fitted in here. How he was going to handle this he hadn't quite decided. He needed to pump Ullrich a little more first.

Lunch with Lois had been an extremely brief affair. On their return from the commissary they found a note on the desk from Ullrich saying he wouldn't be back that afternoon. There was no explanation. Frank hoped for Ullrich's sake the sender of the letters didn't decide this was the time to make good on his threats.

Frank was also well aware of some of the more lurid stories that emanated from the Hollywood press, so he'd asked Lois if Ullrich fancied himself as a ladies' man. She'd taken a moment or two to answer, then said she didn't know, but from the look on her face he knew he'd hit the mark. He stopped short of asking whether he'd tried it on with her, but concluded he hadn't.... yet.

Frank had a lot of experience dealing with people, Ullrich struck him as someone who got his own way on a regular basis, and woebetide anyone who got in his way. The little episode he'd witnessed with the writer the previous day was testament to that, but early days though it was, a picture was beginning to emerge. He turned the La Salle onto Barham and thought some more as he headed back into Hollywood.

Benny was waiting in the office when he got back. He'd been reading a copy of the *Examiner* from the previous week that Ellie had kept in her desk. The murder had been front page news.

"Jesus, Frank, this is just terrible. What the hell happened? The couple in the case worked in a bank. Surely they weren't involved?"

"How did you know that, Benny, it's not in the file?"

"I was with Tony the day he picked up the surveillance. You know Tony, he was always a little behind on his paperwork."

"Yeah, I guess he was," said Frank slowly. "Anyway, the answer's no. Cops checked them out. Clean as a whistle."

Benny sat down with a sigh staring at the headlines as if somehow they might alter. "Says here the car was found out on Mulholland, near the reservoir. What the hell was he doing out there?"

"That's what nobody can figure. Of course it's possible the two lovebirds he was following might have chosen it for their secret rendezvous. It is a popular spot."

"But you said the couple were clean?"

"They were, but maybe he followed the wrong party, or something. We don't know that yet." He paused. "Anyway they don't think that's where he was killed. They don't say in the paper, but his body was in the trunk. So they think the car was driven and dumped where they found him."

Benny's face was pale and his voice sounded strained. "It makes no sense at all. Do you think he stumbled onto something, a heist of some sort, or a kidnapping maybe?"

Frank shook his head slowly.

"According to Brady they checked every possible angle. Nothing else was reported in the area that would give that impression. So whatever it was must still be under wraps."

"You know what they say, Frank," said Benny grimly. "A guy's got to find out who killed his partner."

"Don't worry, Benny, we will."

Benny was quiet for a moment. "Any chance we could go take a look at where it happened? You know, just to give us something to do?"

Frank reached down to a drawer in the desk, produced a quart bottle of Old Plantation, and set two glasses side by side. He poured an inch into each and passed one over to Benny. They drank in silence.

After a moment or two Frank spoke. "Okay. I guess I've been putting this off long enough." He grabbed his hat and went through to the outer office, Benny following in his wake.

"Ellie, we're just going to take a ride over to where they found Tony's car. I'll check with you in the morning before I go back to the studio. By the way can you drop into a bookstore someplace and see if you can pick up anything you can find on quotations?"

Ellie stopped typing. "Sure, Frank, but....."

He'd gone before she could ask why.

Neither man spoke as they headed up Highland to where it merged with Cahuenga and began the climb into the foothills. Ahead to the north-east, high in the scrub-covered hills, a huge white-painted metal sign proclaimed HOLLYWOODLAND, the name of a 500 acre sub-division.

The following morning Lieutenant Brady had both his feet on the desk and a cup of coffee in his hands when Harrigan and Benny appeared in his doorway. It was one of a row of glass-fronted offices along the inner wall of the building with no window to the outside. The only decoration in the room was a large-scale map of Los Angeles County. Brady dropped his feet to the floor and stood up.

"Mr Walsh, isn't it? Take a seat."

"Yes," mumbled Benny in a rather inaudible voice, as he sat on one of the hard wooden chairs opposite the desk. He hadn't really wanted to come down here in the first place: he couldn't see how anything he knew would help catch Tony's killer. Frank had insisted, saying the cops would eventually come looking for him. Visiting the murder site on Mulholland last night had not helped much either. He and Frank had just sat there, each with their own thoughts, staring out across the city at the Pacific and drinking from a flask until darkness fell.

Brady glanced sharply at Harrigan, who took the hint and departed, quietly closing the door.

"Now, Benny. Can I call you Benny?"

"Sure," said Benny, relaxing slightly.

Brady picked up a pencil, pushed the manilla file to one side and placed a yellow pad in front of him. He glanced at the calendar block on his desk, grunted, tore off the top two sheets, then wrote today's date on the pad.

"Now, I want you to tell me all you know about that last week with Tony. Don't leave anything out, because it may be important. We need to find whoever did this

- fast. When you've done, we'll get it typed up for you to sign."

"Could I get a cup of coffee before we start?"

"Sure, sure." Brady held up his cup and signalled through the glass to Harrigan who, muttering under his breath, went off to obey.

Benny, who took his coffee white, decided not to complain when it arrived without any milk. He just closed his eyes and sipped. Brady examined the end of his pencil and waited.

"On the Tuesday," Benny began, "Tony got a call from some guy to say he thought his wife, who worked at the Union Bank on Santa Monica, was seeing another guy. It could be someone she worked with, but he wasn't sure. He wanted some definite evidence. We had strict instructions to be as discreet as possible. He didn't want no scenes. The next couple of days we stake the place out and follow her home. Zilch."

He paused and waited for Brady to finish writing.

"Then on the Thursday she came out at lunchtime, walked about three blocks and went into a diner. A few minutes later this guy shows up and sits in the same booth. So we figure this is him. Tony waits outside, ready to follow the guy when he leaves. I go in and get a coffee at the counter. They eat and there appears to be a fairly animated discussion taking place. I watch them in a mirror on the back wall. After about a half hour he gets up to leave. I stay put and keep watching her. Ten minutes later I follow her back to the Bank."

Brady held up his hand as he turned to a new page, at the same time unwrapping a fresh stick of gum and shoving it into his mouth.

"Okay, carry on," he said, chewing mechanically.

Benny gulped down the rest of the coffee and went on. "When I get back to the car, Tony's already there waiting. Guess what, he says to me, the guy works at the same Bank she does. Surprise, surprise. He has no doubt they are an item. So we sit for a while trying to figure how we're going to catch them... ah... in the act so to speak. Then I remember I used to know a guy who works security there, so I go back and check. He still works there, but he ain't working that day. So I say I'll catch him tomorrow, that's the Friday, which I got to say, is usually Tony's day at the track. And which incidentally he and Frank don't always see eye to eye on."

"Stick to the statement, Benny, please."

"Oh yeah, yeah. You got all that?"

"Sure," said Brady. "Go on."

"That evening I get the call that my sister's in hospital with a broken rib, so I call Tony and tell him I got to go to 'Frisco. But I say I'll talk to this security guy tomorrow and if anything comes up I'll leave a message with the man at his apartment building. Next day I meet the guard on his break and after some chat he tells me half the bank knows this guy's bouncing the chick...."

"The name, the guy's name?"

"Oh yeah, Peters, I think. Works in accounting. Anyway for a few bucks he reveals that, according to the talk around, they usually meet at the boyfriend's place on a Saturday night, and for a few bucks more he gets me an address. Then he grins and says, she must have one damn fancy story to tell her old man. So I leave this information with the super at Tony's address and catch the a.m. bus to 'Frisco."

Brady finished writing and looked up. "That's it?"

"All I can remember."

"What about the address?"

"The address?"

"The one you sent Tony to."

"Oh yeah. Braemont Drive, north of Hollywood Boulevard someplace. I didn't have time to look it up."

"The number. Can you remember the number?"

Benny scratched his head. "It was either four two one or six two one."

"Okay we can check that out. You're sure it was Braemont Drive?"

"Yeah, definitely. Does it matter?"

"Sure it does. Now at least we know where he was supposed to have gone."

Brady scribbled the address down.

"What's going to happen to the car?" asked Benny.

"What car?"

"Tony's car."

"Oh, yeah. It's impounded for evidence at the moment. Why do you ask?"

Benny looked a little sheepish. "Tony only had it a couple of months. He loved that car."

Brady nodded silently and gave a grim smile. It was another half hour before the statement was typed for Benny to sign. Then they said he could go.

After Benny had left Harrigan came into Brady's office carrying a copy of the statement.

"I've read this through, Lieutenant. Doesn't get us much further does it?"

"Well, it gives us the boyfriend's address which we didn't have before, so now we can go check if anyone saw Tony's car there on the night of the murder."

"True, but according to the wife she was home all that night, and the husband backs her up."

"Okay, so maybe nothing happened, but Tony didn't know that. He'd be waiting for them to show."

"We coulda had all this before," said Harrigan "if the wife had given us the boyfriend's name."

"Like hell she was going to admit that, with her husband looking over her shoulder. What was it Benny said in the statement - he thought they were having an animated discussion in the diner?"

"Yeah, something like that. Why?"

"Could be she was ending the affair right there."

"Could be that's why she didn't show on the Saturday."

"Precisely." Brady moved a piece of gum around his mouth. "Looks like we've got all the pieces for the first part of the puzzle, but none for the second. Get moving and check out any sightings of the car in Braemont Drive. Talk to this Peters guy as well and double check his address with the phone company."

"What about the security guard at the bank, should we check him too?"

"Yeah, why not."

Harrigan left and Brady resumed his customary position with his feet on the desk. He still had a few days left before he'd have to report back to Malone. There was still a chance he might pick up a few leads, but time was running out.

7

While Benny was giving his statement to Lieutenant Brady downtown, Frank was studying a copy of Five Thousand Quotations for all Occasions' by some guy called Lewis Henry, which the ever resourceful Ellie had managed to procure from Geiger's bookshop on Hollywood Boulevard near Las Palmas.

He vaguely remembered there had been a case about that a few months back. It had been all over the press. The owner had been involved in some sort of dirty book racket and got himself murdered. The rumour was he'd also done some blackmail on the side. They must be under new management.

"A treasury of wit and wisdom, beauty and sentiment," read the blurb on the front cover. Yeah, sure, thought Frank, and all for seventy five cents.

Subjects were arranged in alphabetical order, so it didn't take long to find the page on death, or to find the sources of the quotes.

Frank snapped the book shut and leaned back in his chair. There didn't seem to be any great conclusion he could draw from this. Only that using someone else's words gave no clue to the personality of the sender, a sort of death threat by proxy. As indeed had been the method of delivery. Something else he'd learned from Lois. Brilliantly simple really, an envelope slipped into the internal mail system, casually dropped in any out-tray on the lot. Impossible to trace. It did tie it down to someone in the studio, which so to speak, narrowed it down to a cast of thousands.

"Boss?" Ellie was standing in the doorway with a cigarette in her mouth.

"Ellie, you don't smoke."

"Well, I just started."

"You go to the movies last night?"

"Yeah. How did you know?"

Frank smiled. "Just a guess."

"The book okay?"

"Splendid."

"You gonna tell me what all this is about?" she said holding the cigarette between her fingers in the best movie star fashion.

Frank flicked at some of his own ash which had dropped onto his carefully pressed white shirt. He'd taken a little bit more time over his dress that morning bearing in mind the role he was about to play. He'd even put a new blade in his Gillette. Although he had to admit that might have had more to do with Lois than anything else. "Well, friend Ullrich has received a couple of threatening letters."

"Threatening letters. . . who from?"

"We don't know that yet, Ellie."

"Maybe it's just a leg-pull. You know what those movie people are like with their practical jokes."

Frank knew Ellie spent lots of her spare time reading movie magazines, cover to cover and probably twice over.

"That's a possibility, but it's gone on a little too long. Maybe someone who wants to make him squirm a little, but there's no way of telling that unless someone owns up, which I doubt."

"So what are you going to do?"

"They want me to go undercover at the studio to see if I can find the culprit."

"Jeez, does that mean you'll be mixing with real movie stars?" said Ellie in wonder.

Frank wasn't sure whether this was Ellie in her small-town girl mode, so he played it straight. "It's possible I'll bump into a few, but don't expect me to get any autographs."

She made a face. "Some people get all the luck."

"Back to business now, Ellie." said Frank. "Did you manage to dig up any more on Ullrich?"

"Not a lot, but he was apparently producing some

play on Broadway when there was some scandal. It was all hushed up and they managed to keep it out of the newspapers. So far I haven't been able to find out exactly what it was, but I'll keep digging."

"Okay, I'm going to take off to the studio. Benny will be back shortly, tell him to hang around. I'll give you a call later and see if I can find something to keep him occupied. Otherwise he'll just sit around and brood about Tony."

"Okay boss," she said. "So long as you don't forget the troops."

Frank went out of the building thinking either Ellie was watching too many movies or she must be taking an evening correspondence course. Perhaps both.

The trip to the studio was uneventful, although Frank kept a wary eye on the rearview mirror, for what he was now sure was a green Plymouth sedan. He'd given a lot of thought as to who might want to put a tail on him. It was a cinch that whoever killed Tony knew by now that he was the other half of the team. That is unless they'd gone to live on a desert island.

Frank was an old hand at the tailing game and knew how to turn the tables if necessary. Meanwhile if they slipped up once he'd have them.

Almost before he realised it he was approaching the studio gate. This time the guard gave him a quick glance and waved him through. He noticed it was the same guy as last time.

Lois looked even better than yesterday, if such a

thing were possible. She wore a well tailored cream suit with a simple round neck white silk blouse. Frank knew if she suggested they take a slow boat to China he'd have gone with what he stood up in.

"Well," she said. "Good morning."

Even those few words were enough to take his breath away. "Yeah, I guess," was all he managed. Frank really did have a great flair for dialogue even if it wasn't displayed on this occasion.

"Mr Ullrich is down in screening room three. He said for you to join him as soon as you came in." She gave him a precise set of instructions on how to get there and watched him leave. "I'll show you your new office when you get back," she called after him.

"I can't wait." he said glancing back.

Frank walked out of the building into the morning sun and tried to get his bearings from the instructions Lois had given him. Warners was a sprawling 135-acre facility which they had aquired on their merger with First National in 1928. The whole area was dominated by at least twenty towering hangar-like sound stages and outdoor sets where most of the filming took place.

Surrounding this was a maze of ancillary buildings required to provide every conceivable means of support. The screening-rooms were one of these. After a couple of wrong turnings Frank found himself outside a building that indicated he'd reached his destination. The large numeral and the wording on the door left him in no doubt.

He entered the darkened building and waited for his eyes to become accustomed to the gloom. There was a projection booth on his left and some double doors in front of him which led into the small theater. A group of five men and one woman, including he supposed Ullrich, were just about discernible down on the front row. A table between the seats held a couple of telephones, a small shaded lamp, and a buzzer to communicate with the projectionist.

Frank took a seat in the back row and waited. There was the occasional flare of a match and long curls of cigarette smoke drifted through the sharp flickering beam of the projector then vanished again into the surrounding darkness.

The action on the screen, in black and white, was taking place in a cafe with different characters and conversations taking place. Then he recognised a close up of Edward G Robinson lighting his pipe in a scene where he was questioning a suspect. His on screen presence was magnetic. Suddenly the screen went white, and the lights came on.

An animated discussion ensued, mostly technical terms which were over Frank's head. It lasted about ten minutes before they all began to move up the aisle.

"Ah," said Ullrich, his face changing when he saw Frank. "You made it. What did you think?"

Frank fell in beside him as they headed toward the exit. He didn't know the first thing about movies and he was quite sure Ullrich didn't really give a damn what he thought either, but still.

"A little hard to judge from such a small clip. Edward G looked terrific, but then he always does."

"They're just the dailies spliced together from the week's shooting, but it's looking pretty good."

A hard-faced woman with shortish blonde hair, who'd been one of the group, gave Frank a somewhat quizzical look before walking off.

Noticing, Ullrich put a hand on his shoulder. "Don't worry about her. That's Linda Salisbury, the unit publicist; there's one on every movie. I haven't got as far as telling her who you are, or rather meant to be."

"Right," said Frank. "What's this film really about?"

Ullrich glanced around before replying. "Just a sort of FBI story. You know, good guys versus bad guys. Oh, by the way this is Milton Feldman, he's my junior associate producer." He jerked a thumb backwards over his shoulder. Frank turned to shake hands with the rather weedy young man with spectacles, a pencil behind his ear and the inevitable script under his arm. He'd been trailing in their wake since they left the screening room. "Frank DeMarco...ah...story consultant," said Frank. As he dropped Feldman's damp hand he couldn't help noticing the carnation in his buttonhole. The youth gave a pale smile, then resumed his position a couple of steps behind.

"Now, Frank," said Ullrich. "One thing I got to ask you to do, and that's not to repeat anything you learn while you are here at the studios. There are hundreds people out there who feed off this industry, that's why we have to have our own publicity department, of which the lady you saw was one. They tell them only what we want them to know and nothing else. That's especially true about this latest movie. Does that come as a surprise to you?"

"Not at all, Mr Ullrich. In my business I'm a long way past being surprised by anything. Tell me though, what makes this movie different from any other?" Frank looked directly at Ullrich and sensed from the look on his face that he wasn't going to get a straight answer to his question.

"Well, let's just say it's highly controversial, and unless I can convince Jack Warner I still may not get to make it exactly the way I want."

Frank digested this for a moment. "You realise this could throw a whole new angle on who might have sent the notes."

"The thought had occurred to me and I can tell you the studio is bracing itself for any repercussions the film might provoke. But very few people know about it at the moment, and the notes struck me as something a good deal more personal."

Frank figured that was about as far as Ullrich was going to go for the time being. "Okay," he said. "It's your call, but I think you should keep the possibilty in mind.

They walked on for a few moments in silence. Suddenly they were surrounded by a milling crowd of

MULHOLLAND DRIVE

extras all wearing U.S. cavalry uniforms. For a moment, in the general melee, Frank lost sight of Ullrich. He suddenly realised how easy it would be for someone to get into the studios as an extra, knife a victim and disappear into the crowd before anyone knew. The swarm passed and he saw Ullrich standing several yards away. By the look on his face the thought had also occurred to him.

"Just as well none of them were after you, but it does demonstrate the scale of the problem."

Ullrich managed a grim smile.

Frank went on. "By the way, I found the real authors of the quotes your joker used in the threats. The first one was from *Macbeth,* although they changed the tense, the second was Oscar Wilde."

"Well I suppose I ought to be flattered that someone should go to such lengths. Do you think that suggests someone with a literary mind, a writer perhaps?"

"I'm afraid there's a rather more mundane reason than that. You can pick them out of a seventy-five cent book, and they don't give any clue to the sender. Still, if it's any consolation, this is Hollywood and you are among the most creative minds in the country."

Ullrich gave another grim smile. "That is a comforting thought," he said.

Perhaps, mused Frank, there might be something in that. A knife in the back might be altogether too unimaginative for someone who thought in terms of Shakespeare and Wilde. They might be planning something much more spectacular in the way of an exit for their victim. First chance he had he'd check Ullrich's diary to see if there were any occasions that would afford such an opportunity. He decided to keep the thought to himself for the moment.

As they walked along Ullrich gave him a running commentary on the functions of each of the buildings they passed from cutting rooms to carpentry. Amazingly they managed to arrive back at the front office without bumping into any stars. Ellie just wasn't going to believe it.

8

The Warner commissary was divided into three sections. The first was the exclusive executive dining room; the second for directors, producers and stars; and the last and largest for movie crews, extras and staff. There were hundreds of wood tables and a long serving counter. The style was a sort of late hacienda.

"Now," Lois said firmly. "It's my turn to ask the questions."

She smiled sweetly across at Frank. They were sitting by the window, this time eating club steaks.

"Fire away," he said.

"How, exactly, does a man get into an occupation like yours?"

Frank put down his fork and sipped from the glass of seltzer water, wishing it was mixed with something stronger.

"It's a long story, but briefly I started out in the LAPD, then moved up to the DA's office as an investigator. At first it seemed like a step in the right direction, but then things are never quite what they seem. What it comes down to is there are only so many times you can look the other way, before it becomes a habit. After a couple of years I figured I'd better get out before I turned into someone I didn't like."

Lois arched an eyebrow. "Well, that does sound rather depressing. If we can't trust the police department, who can we trust?"

"People join the department for lots of different reasons, some good some bad. That doesn't mean there aren't a lot of honest cops around, because there are. It just make their job a little harder. But I wouldn't blame them too much, it's the politicians who really run things, been that way a long time now."

"You still haven't said why you choose to become a private detective?"

"After the police and the DA's office the alternatives do become a little limited."

Lois dabbed her mouth with a napkin.

"Sounds a bit like the movie business."

Frank's eyes widened slightly.

"Oh," she said. "I don't mean in a criminal sense. But you don't have to be in this business for long to see the lengths the studios will go to protect their image. And, of course, the stars."

"Ullrich did mention something this morning about publicity control, but I didn't take it too seriously."

"Well, believe me, *they* do. Can you imagine what would happen if someone like Errol Flynn were to get arrested for being drunk, or, dare one say it, rape? The publicity could finish him. It wouldn't do the studio much good either. Think of that in terms of dollars and cents."

"Yeah, I'm beginning to get the idea. When you walk through those studio gates, it's like entering another world."

"Believe me it really is another world, and subject to the rule of one man."

They were both silent for a few minutes while they finished eating. Frank studied that exquisite profile out of the corner of his eye. There was no doubt she was tough, sophisticated and sure of herself. He tried to figure out what she might be thinking, instead he'd begun to notice flecks of hazel in those big blue eyes.

"What about you?" he said. "How long have you been working for Ullrich?"

"Oh, about six months."

"Where are you from originally?"

"A small town in Indiana."

"Long way from home. What brought you to Hollywood?"

"What brings any girl to Hollywood?"

Frank smiled. He knew perfectly well what brought most girls to Hollywood, but he was willing to bet none of them applied to Lois. "Fame and fortune I guess," he said.

"That and other things. I thought I'd just come and see what all the fuss was about. So far it's been fun, but the jury's still out. I've seen a little of what happens to all those hopefuls who sign on at Central Casting with the dream of becoming a star and the price they're going to have to pay for it."

Frank wasn't sure but he thought he detected a hint of bitterness in her voice at that last remark. Could it be she was talking from some sort of personal experience?

"Would you like a cup of coffee?" she was saying.

"Sure. Why not?"

Lois rose and and walked back over to the counter. Frank's eyes followed her every step of the way, there and back. There was an amused look in her eyes when she sat down. "You look at all the girls that way?"

"Some," he smiled, reaching into his pocket. "Mind if I smoke?"

"Not at all, go ahead."

Frank lit the cigarette and wondered again what was going on behind that beautiful face. "By the way, I believe it's you I have to thank for getting this job?"

"Well, yes," she laughed. "But I do have a small confession to make."

"What's that?"

"You were my second choice."

"Oh, who was your first?"

"Some guy called Marlowe, but he was involved in a case."

Frank gave a long grin.

"What's that for?"

"I was just thinking what he's missing."

Lois smiled a long cool smile, crossed her nylon clad legs and sipped again at her coffee. "So what's the next step?" she asked in an amused voice.

Frank blew some smoke into the air and tried very hard to concentrate. "I think it's time I met the writing team on this movie. See if they are fans of Shakespeare and Wilde."

"A little obvious, don't you think?"

"You never can tell, but I got to start some place. What are these guys like?"

"Greenberg and Field? Well, that was Greenberg you saw the other day, so that might give you some idea. They seem very friendly, but to be honest no-one knows a lot about them. They arrived about two months ago especially to work on this script. I think someone said they came from New York."

"Really. Isn't that where Ullrich came from originally?"

"Did he tell you that?"

"No, but we have done a little checking on him. This all might stem from his past."

"Yes, I suppose it could," Lois said carefully. "Did you find out much?"

Frank hadn't quite figured out her position in the

scheme of things, or her exact relationship with Ullrich, if there was one, so he just shrugged.

"Not a lot, so far. Just that he produced a show on Broadway. But we'll keep trying. Talking about Ullrich, he seemed to go all cagey when I asked him about this new movie. What's the big deal?"

"Well I don't know all that much about it myself. He always keeps the script under lock and key, such as it is. I have, on occasion, typed up some alterations, but you can't tell much from that. I do know we're due to have a visit soon from some former FBI agent. That might tell you something."

"Any idea who he is?"

"As a matter of fact I do, a rather odd name really. Someone called Leon Turrou."

"Hmm...I'm sure I've heard that name before somewhere." Frank looked thoughtful. "Maybe it's his experiences in the FBI, although I gather Hoover doesn't like his former agents telling tales. That could stir up some trouble but I doubt if that would explain the notes."

"You're the detective." She grinned, glancing at her watch. "Heavens, look at the time. I'd better be getting back, they're pretty strict on time keeping you know. I can't afford to lose my job. I'll show you your office on the way."

The office was on the ground floor of the writers' block. The most important thing in it was the telephone which she had assured him was a direct line and didn't go through the studio switchboard. The last thing he wanted was anyone eavesdropping on his calls. There was also an internal telephone along with a complete staff list which, according to Lois, was updated and retyped every month. His first task would be to go through it and mark out people who had direct contact with Ullrich. It was only a starting point, but they would be first on his "most likely" list.

The internal phone at his elbow rang.

"Hello?"

"Mr DeMarco," came Ullrich's booming voice. "How is your new office?"

"Just fine."

"Lois tells me it's a little small."

"I'll survive. I don't figure on spending a lot of time in it."

"Good. Look, since I gather from Lois you worked in the DA's office, I thought your cover might be better as a consultant on investigative procedure and the overall look of the movie. How does that strike you?"

"Sounds fine to me."

"Great. Now there's a production meeting in half an hour I'd like you to come. Most of the people on the movie will be there. I'll just give you an offhand introduction and after that you're on your own. You'll have a chance to cast your eye over everybody, but there won't be any formal introductions so you'll have to pick up names as you go along. Okay?"

"Sure. How will I find this place?"

"I'll send Lois down a few minutes before to take you there."

"Right," said Frank as he hung up. Nothing like plunging in at the deep end. At least it would give him a chance to observe everyone while their attention was directed elsewhere.

Ullrich certainly hadn't wasted any time pumping Lois on their lunchtime conversation. Still, if it added to his credibility, it couldn't do much harm. Though he'd have to remember that in future conversations.

Lois left him at the door of the meeting room. About fifteen people in various modes of dress, were standing around chatting, then Ullrich strode into the room and took a seat midway down the long wooden table.

"Mr Ullrich," said Feldman, the junior associate producer. "Don't you want to sit at the head of the table?"

Ullrich looked up from his papers. "Son, wherever I sit *is* the head of the table."

Feldman sat down, his face rather flushed.

"Ah, Frank." Ullrich waved his hand. "Folks, this is Frank DeMarco - used to work in the DA's office. He's going to advise us on any details of procedure etc that we might encounter on the movie. Now to business."

Frank sank into an empty chair, as several heads of those now seated swivelled in his direction. Most hadn't given him anything other than a bored glance, but he was aware of a more direct look from Linda the woman publicist he'd seen that morning at the screening.

Her hair looked like it was set permanently and her body had a lean hardness to it, evident even this far away. From this distance she was not unattractive, close up might be a different story, probably on her third husband though.

The meeting droned on for a while, most of what they were talking about went straight over Frank's head. There seemed to be a fairly heated argument going on regarding the delays in filming certain sequences. Some of the ire was directed at the writers who defended themselves admirably, but most appeared to be accounts of unexplained equipment failure and other unspecified problems involving some of the cast.

Frank let all this wash over him as he scrutinized each member of the team in turn. They certainly were an assorted bunch, who knew what grudges and resentments they might be harbouring. He'd picked up a few names, but he could get the rest from Lois later. It was well after five when the meeting broke up.

9

Frank sipped his tomato juice and scanned the front page of the *Los Angeles Examiner*. He was sitting in the window booth of Hal's Diner on Franklin, a couple of blocks from his apartment. On the rare occasions when he woke up without a hangover this was where he usually ate breakfast.

The news continued to get more depressing by the day. Europe was sliding inexorably into war. As it did the voices of pacifism, including W. R. Hearst himself, became even more strident. Everybody knew of Hearst's anti-British views: he expressed them often enough. What only a few knew, however, was that Hearst's empire was crumbling and large parts were being sold off to finance massive debts. What even fewer people knew was across town RKO studios were preparing a thinly-disguised exposé of the great press baron to be called *Citizen Kane*, which, when it was finally released, would practically destroy Hearst.

Frank figured if half the world was intent on going to hell in a hand-basket, America could not stand on the sidelines for long. It was another report though, from New York, which troubled him a whole lot more.

The previous evening twenty-two thousand people had attended a German-American Bund rally in Madison Square Garden to be addressed by some nut wearing a Nazi uniform. Photographs showed the Stars and Stripes hanging alongside the black and red swastika of Nazi Germany. Frank didn't spent a lot of time thinking about politics. That's what they sent those guys to Washington for, wasn't it? Let's hope they could deal with it.

He folded the paper in disgust as the waitress arrived with his ham and eggs.

"That all?" she said as she poured the coffee.

"Thank you, yes."

She scribbled out the check from a pad hanging at her waist, folded it and slid it under his plate. Then walked off with an exaggerated swing of her hips.

Fifteen minutes later he was back in the LaSalle and heading downtown for the office, his own that is, not the one at the studio.

It was 8.45 am on a bright clear morning in February, 1939 and the rest of the world and its insanity seemed a million miles away. Although the sun was warm the air had a distinct chill, this was after all what passed for winter in Los Angeles. Brief though it was, it signalled the fashion conscious of Hollywood who never tired of parading the Boulevard in their tweed jackets, argyle sweaters, and two-tone brogues.

Frank checked the rearview mirror automatically for any uninvited guests. Either they were getting clever and using a different car or they'd pegged him and decided on a stakeout. He circled the block a couple of times, just to be sure, but didn't spot anybody. He parked, went into the building, and waited for the elevator.

Ellie stood up as he entered the office, jerked her finger at the inner door, and mouthed what looked like "Brady."

Frank nodded his understanding, walked into the room and threw his hat on the stand. "Well, what brings you over here, Phil? Running out of suspects again?"

Brady, who was seated on the divan chewing gum and reading the newspaper, spoke quietly. "I already apologised for that, Frank, wasn't it enough?"

"Yeah, yeah," said Frank, holding up his hands. "I guess I just got out of the wrong side of bed this morning."

Brady smiled faintly and glanced around. "This place hasn't changed much since I was here last. You could still do with some new linoleum."

Frank grunted and sat down at the desk. "Is that a paper I see you reading?"

Brady folded the newspaper and put it down by his side. "Yeah, surprise, surprise. You read any of this front page stuff?" he said.

Frank blinked. "You mean all that Nazi rally shit in New York? Yeah, one hopes it's just a one day wonder."

"Don't be too sure, we've got some of those bastards right here in L.A."

"You're kidding?"

"Far from it. We've even sent some of our guys undercover to one of their meetings, see if we can find out what they're up to."

"How come we ain't read about any of this?"

"We've been doing our best to keep the lid on it, that's why, but this New York affair has brought it all out into the open."

As if by telepathy Ellie appeared with a couple of mugs of coffee. Frank sat back in his chair and looked across at Brady as he drank.

"So what's this all about? You sure as hell didn't come all this way to discuss the world situation, or the state of my lino."

A thin smile touched Brady's lips. "No, that's true. I thought you'd like to know that we've checked Benny's statement over with a toothcomb and the bottom line is, it puts you virtually in the clear."

"Virtually?"

"If you want it spelled out, it's highly improbable, but not utterly impossible."

"That's a pleasant and comforting start to the day.

What changed your mind?"

"It wasn't my mind that needed changing, Frank, if you recall, but that of a certain Captain."

"Right. What changed his mind?"

"Well, according to Benny, Tony spent the Friday at the track, something you didn't know about. Benny then left a message for Tony with the super at his apartment building that afternoon, but since Tony didn't get back until late evening it was passed on by the night man. You follow?"

"Sure. What was the message?"

"The address for the stakeout on Braemont Drive off Laurel Canyon Boulevard, where the broad from the bank was supposed to meet her fancy man."

"So did Tony go there?"

"Not so far as we can tell. We've checked the neighbourhood out throughly and there's no evidence to suggest he ever went near the place. I checked with the night man at Tony's apartment building, according to him Tony went out that evening about seven-thirty, said he was on a job and would be back late. Exactly where he went from there is still a mystery. We're checking all the bars and clubs in the neighbourhood for another sighting. But nothing yet."

Frank finished off his coffee. "I really appreciate your coming by, Phil, it takes a weight off my mind. I'm on another case now and haven't had much chance to follow things up. But if I'm any judge finding that last link is going to be tough."

Brady got up, walked across the room and put his hand on the door. "Always is, Frank, always is. But, as you said before, that's what the city pays us for, so we won't be giving up yet awhile." He opened the door. "You come across anything, you will let me know?"

"Sure thing, buddy," Frank came around the desk. "You forgot your paper." He picked it up and pushed it under Brady's arm. "If what my guts are telling me is right, it might not be long before you and I will be out there fighting a different kind of war."

Brady didn't reply, but raised the paper as he crossed the outer office and smiled across at Ellie. "Be seeing you, kiddo," he said.

Frank stood for a moment in the doorway and watched him disappear down the hall. "Well I guess things are back to some reasonable semblance of normality," he said to Ellie. "At least on one front. Anything to report before I head off to the studio?"

"Not a lot. I've got an agency tracking down anything that may have happened to any of the cast on the New York show, but since it ran for several months, it's a long period to cover."

"Right," said Frank. "What about the writers Greenberg and Field I asked you to check yesterday?"

"Oh yes, they worked on the play with Ullrich. But there's no hint so far of any problems."

He was just about to ask about Benny when the phone rang. Ellie picked it up.

"Senna and DeMarco. Ah...yes, Miss Cain, he is

here, I'll put him on."

She passed the phone to Frank.

"Hello, Lois." He listened in silence. "Okay. Do nothing, I'll be out right away."

He handed the phone back to Ellie with a grim look. "They've had another threatening letter."

10

Frank made the studio in slightly over half an hour, pushing the speed limit and running a few lights on the way. He just hoped he hadn't been spotted by any sharp-eyed highway cops.

Lois looked up quickly and gave him a pale smile when he walked into her office.

"You can go right in," she said.

Frank nodded, but tapped on the door before going through. Ullrich was pacing about like a caged animal. There was a bottle of Seagrams Seven Crown whiskey on his desk, and a grim expression on his face.

"Mr DeMarco, thank you for coming so promptly. Would you like a drink? I hate drinking alone."

"Just a small one, thanks."

Ullrich poured two drinks and handed one to Frank.

Without any further word he slid the note across the desk. Frank sat down and studied it quietly as Ullrich continued to pace nervously about. In a couple of gulps Ullrich drained his glass and quickly poured himself another.

The note was completely different in every way imaginable from the previous two. First, it was on some cheap notepaper torn from a yellow ruled pad and second, no melodramatic cut-out lettering or quotes from the Bard this time. It was simply typed in caps, and fairly badly at that. It read:

IF THIS MOVIE EVER APPEARS
ON THE SCREEN, YOU WILL NOT
BE AROUND TO SEE IT.

Frank looked at it for a few more minutes.

"How did this arrive?"

"In the mail. It was marked personal, so Lois left it on my desk for me to open when I came in, which was just before she called you."

"Let me get this straight, you're talking about the normal mail and not the internal mail?"

"Correct." Ullrich handed over the torn envelope. "Postmarked Los Angeles, yesterday."

"Well now, Mr Ullrich," said Frank slowly. "It looks to me like we might have a whole new ball game here. This is about as far from those other two notes as you can get."

Ullrich finally sat down, his face drawn.

"Are you saying I've got two different people threatening my life?"

"Let's not leap to conclusions yet. What I mean is we now have a far more specific threat, and one that is tied to the new movie. The other two were vague and melodramatic and at a pinch could have been laughed off as a joke. This very definitely can't."

Ullrich finished off the rest of his drink, and nervously picked a cigar from the humidor on his desk. "So, you think it is two different people?"

"There's no way of telling at this stage. It could of course be a deliberate ploy to keep you off balance. It's hard to accept that it could all be just a coincidence. Or maybe they thought a more direct attack would show they meant business."

Ullrich stood up, walked to the window, and stared out for some moments. He looked less like the all powerful movie producer than Frank had so far seen. "What do you suggest we do now?" he said harshly.

"What you have to do, Mr Ullrich, is to tell me exactly what this movie is about and why precisely someone out there should want to go to these lengths to stop it."

Ullrich sat down heavily and sighed. Finally he lit the corona cigar he'd been playing with. "I suppose you would have to find out sooner or later. Ever hear of a man named Leon Turrou?"

"No," lied Frank. Lois had mentioned his name, but there was no point in involving her in the discussion.

"Well precisely one year ago Mr Turrou, then an agent for the FBI, was called in by Army Intelligence to try and locate a Nazi spy ring in New York. He succeeded, which led to the arrest and trial of those involved. It was in all the newspapers at the time, although I'm not sure what coverage it received here."

"I can't say as I recall," confessed Frank.

"Then the *New York Post* approached him to write a series of articles about the affair, which he did. But he was promptly dismissed by FBI Director Hoover who doesn't like his agents claiming personal success."

"I can see where Hoover might have been a bit peeved at that. So, let me guess, you're making a movie out of this story?"

"Right. I was working in New York at the time and when I came out here I sold Jack Warner on the idea, he's very keen on stories from the headlines. He was a little wary, though, the situation in Europe being what it is, but since the murder of the Warner representative in Berlin, some months back, he's been all for it."

"So unless Hoover himself has started sending out threatening letters that only leaves us with Nazi sympathizers. Or of course," said Frank deliberately, "the Nazis themselves."

Ullrich had gone two shades paler in the last few moments. "Did you have someone in mind?"

Frank rubbed his chin. "I take it from that you haven't seen your papers this morning?"

"Well no, with all this letter business I haven't had a

chance." He pressed his intercom button. "Lois, can you bring in the morning papers?"

A few minutes later he was staring at those same headlines Frank had read that morning. When he looked up his eyes were hard. "Do you think we got any of those types around here?"

"Oh yeah," said Frank. "All over."

"You mean even here at the studio?"

"No reason why not."

"That might explain a couple of things."

"What things?"

Ullrich shrugged. "That's not important right now. What we've got to decide is where we go from here."

Frank knew there was something Ullrich was keeping back, but he decided not to push him on it for the moment.

"You don't have much choice, unless you want to close the movie down and let those bastards win."

"That isn't, of course, wholly my decision."

"You mean it's Jack Warners?"

"Yes."

"So he knows about this note?"

"He does."

"What was his reaction?"

"Well, if you knew Jack Warner you'd probably guess. He's not the sort of man to give in to threats. All he said was if I wanted off the picture, that was fine. He'd find someone else to continue."

Frank sat back and finished his drink. "So really it's a

question of whether you yourself go on, then?"

Ullrich sighed. Frank could sense the immense pressure he was under.

"Right," said Ulrich. "Screw them."

Frank stood up. "I take that means business as usual?"

Ullrich seemed much more like his old self and actually smiled. "It does," he said.

If Ullrich was happier, thought Frank as he left the room, perhaps it was because he thought he knew exactly who his enemies were. Mind you that wouldn't help a great deal if you couldn't actually identify them.

Lois looked up as he came into her office. "How did it go?" she asked anxiously.

"We go on as normal for the time being. For what it is worth since the threat now appears to be tied to the release of the movie there doesn't appear to be any immediate danger, but you never can tell."

"Does this make your job any easier?"

"Not really, but now we know it's connected with the picture and not personal, we can narrow things down a little." Frank noticed she still looked a little pale. "You all right?"

"Yes, fine, really. I've got you a plan of the studio so you can find your way around. I've marked the sound stages where the movie is being shot."

"Thanks. By the way, can I have a look at Ullrich's appointments? I'd like to check a hunch."

"Certainly," she said, passing across a brown leather

covered diary. He was just scanning it when Ullrich appeared in the doorway of his office.

"What's so interesting about my diary?"

"Well, prior to today's note I figured your man might be planning your final scene in dramatic fashion, maybe that's changed, but I see no point in dropping your guard. This reception at the Vermont on Friday. What's that for?"

"Just a publicity event connected with the new movie. I'd quite forgotten about it, that's Linda Salisbury's department. You know the lady you saw at the screening."

"Will everyone be there?"

"Yes, I think so," said Ullrich. "They never usually miss the chance of a free meal." He looked at Frank grimly. "I know what you're thinking. Our friend might also figure this is too good a chance for him to miss."

"Better safe than sorry."

"Perhaps you should be there. After all, you're supposed to be on the movie. Lois will be there; she can take care of you. Do you have a tuxedo?"

"I'm afraid I don't get much call for one on this job."

"No problem. Lois will fix you up with a visit to wardrobe. I'm off to watch a screen test. Don't worry Mr DeMarco, I'll watch my back."

11

The writers' block, a three-story building, painted white like most of the buildings on the lot, was tucked away behind the front office in a tree-shaded courtyard. This was where they'd given Frank his tiny office on the ground floor, being the only sort of space that became vacant on a fairly regular basis.

In his short experience with the movies he was beginning to learn that writers seemed to be a law unto themselves. A law which, according to Lois, frequently got them dismissed in fairly short order. Their list of transgressions was endless, from being caught sleeping off their hangovers to taking Jack Warner's name in vain. The latter was all the more popular since he had imposed strict nine to five timekeeping on all the writers, then having someone come around to check on them.

Frank had discovered from the receptionist, that the writers for 'Spies Over America' (the working title of the movie) were in Room 312 on the third floor. He decided it was about time he confronted the obvious suspects.

The third floor was similar to the first, a long central corridor, the only daylight spilling through the reeded glass partioned offices on either side. From all around came the murmur of voices punctuated by the occasional expletive, along with the incessant clatter of typewriters.

There was a piece of black card taped to the door with two names crudely lettered on it: Greenberg and Field. Which alluded to the rather transitory nature of their occupation.

He raised his hand to knock when suddenly the door was whipped open.

"Aha. I thought I saw someone lurking out there. To what do we owe this rather dubious pleasure?"

The speaker was a shortish, intense looking, young man with dark brown hair brushed back, and very bright blue eyes. He wore a pink striped shirt, open at the neck, with the sleeves rolled up.

"You may recall Mr Ullrich introduced me at yesterday's production meeting. . . Frank DeMarco."

"Oh," he said. "I thought you might be one of those guys Jack and Harry send round to see if we're hard at work earning our paycheck."

Frank grinned. "Watch out, I may be doing that next week."

The other man, who looked slimmer and taller and wore a small, rather crooked bow tie, glanced up from his typewriter, flicked up a finger and peered through his heavy black-framed glasses.

"Yeah, I remember you," he said. "You were waiting in Ullrich's outer office the other day, when we were exchanging insults. I never forget a face. Then you turned up at yesterday's production meeting. I'm Bert, by the way, and this is Al. What can we do for you?"

"Friend Ullrich suggested I introduce myself to everyone on the movie, especially yourselves in case you needed any help in writing about police or investigative procedure. He wants to make sure the movie has a really authentic look."

Al, the shorter one, returned to his seat on the opposite side of the pair of beat-up wooden desks and regarded Frank through narrowed eyes. "Just how do you propose to do that?"

"Well, I spent three years as an investigator in the District Attorney's office and before that some years in homicide department. Maybe I can be of some help."

"So what exactly do you do now?" queried Bert.

This wasn't exactly taking the conversation where Frank wanted it to go. "Oh, just a freelance security consultant." He lied with the absolute authority that comes from years of experience in getting the answer you want in the fastest way possible.

"Are you sure that's the only reason you're here?" said Al suspiciously.

Frank decided the best form of defence in this case was attack; he had to push these guys just a little. Get them on the defensive.

"Now just what else is happening here that makes you think there'd be another reason?"

"Did we say anything was happening?" Bert looked wide-eyed across at Al. "Not us. We keep our noses clean, never take Jack Warner's name in vain, not where he's around anyway, and make sure we're here on Fridays."

"Why Fridays?"

"That's when they come around with the paychecks."

Frank smiled soothingly. "I'm sure that's all true. But I'll bet there's nothing goes on at this studio that you guys don't know about. So I'm assuming you are aware of the sudden accidents that have been holding up and spoiling some of the shooting on the movie."

"Well, they mentioned that at the meeting but....."

"Given the subject of this movie," pressed on Frank. "Which I won't mention to your delicate ears, I think Ullrich got me here as a consultant, but was secretly worried that someone might be trying a little sabotage...." He let the sentence hang.

"So he thought you might be handy to have around if things got sort of nasty?" Bert finished.

"There you go, I knew you guys had this all figured out the moment I walked in here."

Both faces broke into smiles.

"Maybe not the first moment." said Al.

"Probably the second," rejoined Bert.

"Now we got all that fencing out of the way, what can you guys tell me about our mutual friend Ullrich?"

Bert and Al looked at each other.

"Who said this guy wasn't smart." said Al.

"I didn't say he wasn't smart." said Bert. "It must have been someone else."

Frank realised their double-act was a form of defence, giving them time to think, and making sure whatever one said the other would back him up.

"You didn't answer my question," persisted Frank.

"The answer is, not a helluva lot," replied Al. "We worked with him in New York about a year or so back doing some rewrites on a play he was producing. When he left for Hollywood, we never expected to see him again. That didn't leave us in tears exactly, we weren't bosom pals. He kept saying our characters weren't vivid enough."

"Yeah, so we wrote in they should all wear plaid shirts, and he didn't even get the joke."

"I have to say fellas," said Frank skeptically. "I'm not sure I would have either, but go on."

"Well, just that we were surprised, let's say very surprised, to get a summons out here to work on this movie."

"Then again maybe not," added Al. "The rate they go through writers in this place we'll soon be out on Hollywood Boulevard with a tin cup."

"Oh, I thought Ullrich seemed like a fairly reasonable

guy." said Frank, trying to provoke some reaction.

"Are you kidding. He's a prize-winning shit and he has a shelf full of awards to prove it. But then," Bert added philosophically, "so is every other producer I ever met."

Al nodded vigorously. "God knows how long the other two guys lasted, but you can bet the bastard's got another team of writers waiting to take our place at this very minute."

Frank puzzled for a moment. "If you use so many writers who gets the credit for writing the script?"

"Who the hell wants credit on this picture? The chances are Adolf will have us all hanging by our balls the moment it's released."

Frank looked slightly confused. "So why are you doing it?"

"They made us an offer we couldn't refuse."

"What was that?"

"Money," said Al, putting on a grave face. "Not, I might add, a great deal of money but...."

"It only goes to show," interrupted Bert, "how cheaply we can be bought."

Frank grinned. These guys must have been watching too many Marx Brothers pictures. However, there was a much more important question he wanted answered. "I gather Ullrich is something of a ladies' man?" he said casually.

"We wouldn't know anything about that," said Al quickly, glancing across at his partner.

"I'll tell you one thing," said Bert. "He sure as hell knows how to pick a secretary. My fantasies will never be the same again."

"Yeah," grumbled Al. "Our secretaries don't look like that. Producers get all the luck."

"Not to mention the money," added Bert solemnly.

Frank decided to change the subject. He didn't want to lose the slight edge he felt he had up to now. "Getting back to the accidents on the set, can you tell me what happened?"

"Oh well, mostly small things," volunteered Al. "Like moving props around the set, so footage shot one day didn't match with the next, and changing the lighting positions which means everything is held up while they re-light the set. Then the cast get all uptight and so on. The worst was the triple klieg light which fell the other day. Dropped twenty feet, coulda killed someone."

"And you don't think that was an accident?"

"Who knows? But putting everything together it sure smells fishy to me."

"And that makes two of us," agreed Bert.

"Okay, I'd appreciate it if you guys kept your lip buttoned on this. We don't want to frighten anyone just yet."

"Why sure thing, Cap'n," said Al springing up and giving a mock salute. "You can count on us."

"I guess I'll see you guys on Friday at the reception, judging by today it looks like being a barrel of laughs."

※ ※ ※

Frank was in a thoughtful mood as he drove the LaSalle back to Hollywood. Just as well he'd heard about the problems on the set at yesterday's production meeting. It had given him the extra cover he needed to start asking questions and divert attention from his real purpose. Mind you, those two seemed to spend so much time trying to prove one was as smart as the other it probably never occured to them he was anything other than what he said he was.

On the face of it Greenberg and Field had looked as innocent as a pair of new-born babes, but Frank had caught that sharp look when he asked about Ullrich being a ladies' man. It was a dollar to a dime, he mused, they knew all about whatever scandal had gone on back there in New York. Added to that either one of them could be harbouring a grudge against Ullrich and using the other for cover. Frank wasn't at all sure that this part of the investigation was relevant now, but things had a habit of smacking you in the mouth if you took anything for granted.

It was nearing three when he parked in his usual spot and went into the building. A heavily built man, in a dark suit, brown fedora pulled well down, exited the elevator as he approached. Frank gave him no more than a casual glance as he got into the car.

As soon as he reached the door to the office he knew something was wrong. It stood slightly ajar and there were a couple of long cracks in the glass panel. His face showing immediate concern, he slipped the .38 from his shoulder holster and listened. No sound came from inside. He eased back the hammer on the .38, pushed silently on the door, and stepped into the room.

"My God, Ellie," he breathed.

She lay crumpled on her side on the floor, dark hair spread around like a halo. He dropped to one knee and touched her neck, she was still breathing. He crossed the office in two silent strides and flung open the inner door. The room was empty but someone had obviously been busy, files and their contents were scattered across the floor.

He holstered his gun, picked Ellie up carefully and carried her to the leatherette settee under the window. Her hair fell back as he laid her down and he saw the ugly bruise behind her ear. She lay pale and motionless as he took a bottle from the desk, poured some Scotch into a glass and trickled it between her lips. After a moment she spluttered, her head jerked and she came to.

"Frank," she gasped. Her eyes opening wide.

"Okay angel, easy."

She groaned, her hand reaching for the bruise. "Wha... what happened?"

"That's just what I was going to ask you."

She sipped some more of the whisky. "I...I just came back from lunch, the... the glass was broken, I opened the door and...and that's all I remember."

"You got sapped, that's what, angel. Somebody was doing a little breaking and entering, you obviously disturbed them."

Ellie sat up and noticed the files scattered all over the floor.

"Good heavens, Frank, did they take anything?"

"No idea until I check, but don't worry about that. I'm going to call a cab and send you home. You can take tomorrow off and have the week-end to recover. Come back Monday if you're okay."

Half-an hour later when Ellie had gone and he'd picked everything off the floor he called the glass company. They'd be across in an hour to replace the door panel, it would take a little longer to get a sign-writer. At least he wouldn't have to worry any more about removing Tony's name.

He poured himself some scotch and sat back in his chair. First the tail, then this. He certainly appeared to have excited someone's interest, but who were they and what were they looking for? Was it connected to Tony or Ullrich? So far as he could tell there was nothing missing from the files, maybe that was because he didn't *have* what they were looking for.... he wasn't quite sure whether that was a good thing or a bad thing.

He knew one thing though, the bastard who sapped Ellie had better start booking dental appointments. He was going to need a lot of them.

12

It was 7.48 am when Sergeant Harrigan finished giving out the day's assignments to the squad. He looked up from his clipboard and checked the clock.

"Oh, one last thing before you go. The Lieutenant here would like to say a few words."

Brady stood up, put a folder on the desk, took the thin cigar out of his mouth and glanced around the room.

"Now, you all know that it's nearly two weeks since the Senna homicide and we're running out of time. The DA's office is putting us under a lot of pressure, not to mention the Chief." He held up his hand. "Okay, so what else is new?"

He held up a department photograph of Senna's body stuffed in the trunk of his car. The back of his head was missing. "I want you to take another look at this. Not a pretty sight, you'll agree."

There was a murmur round the room.

Brady went on. "Now just to recap, we know all Senna's movements up until 8.25 on the night of the killing, when he left Mario's Italian restaurant on Sunset. That's all we've been able to pick up in the last couple of days. From there we imagine he would have gone to the stakeout on Braemont Drive, but he never arrived. At least there's no corroborative evidence to prove that he did. Driving time would only have been around fifteen minutes, but to get to where the body was found is more than thirty five."

He looked out at the rows of silent faces. "The point is, something or someone caused him to change his destination. Or of course have it changed for him. Now that someone may or may not have been his killer. So I want you to make contact with every one of your people on the street for a sighting of either Senna or his car, a 1936 tan Chevy convertible. The license plate is 7-H9."

"Okay, you get all that down," bawled Harrigan.

"Yeah, sarge," came the ragged reply.

"Right. Let's get to it."

The officers filed out of the room with their usual clamour. Brady watched them go with a grim smile. This was his last chance for a break. The Captain's deadline ran out today, and if he knew Malone, he'd be re-assigned and any hope he had of catching Tony's killer would have gone.

About eleven-fifteen Harrigan was at his desk when the telephone rang. It was the despatcher.

"Sarge, I got Murphy on the radio for you, I'll patch him through."

Murphy's voice came over the telephone. "Sarge?"

"Yeah," yelled Harrigan. "Go ahead."

"I'm out here on Claymont and these are all mostly new properties. Six twenty-one looks like it's never been occupied. Why would this guy Senna want to stake out an empty house?"

"Murphy, you dumb mick, the address is supposed to be Braemont not Clay....." Harrigan stopped a minute and shook his big head, his brow began to furrow. "You still there, Murphy?"

"Yeah, sarge."

"Okay, stay put. I'll get back to you."

Brady was in his office drinking coffee his feet on a drawer pulled out from the desk. He was reading a case folder when Harrigan came in.

"Lieutenant, this may not be anything, but Murphy just radioed in from six twenty-one Claymont Drive, which before you say anything, is the wrong address but....."

"How the fuck did he manage that?"

"Well, this is Murphy's first day back since he was off sick, so he never heard any details about the case before this morning's briefing."

Brady shook his head in disbelief. "So what exactly are you saying?"

"You know the address was passed from Benny Walsh to the day manager who we checked, but it was the night man who actually passed it on to Senna. What if he misheard, like Murphy?"

Brady dropped his feet to the floor and sat up.

"Hmm..... bit of a long shot, but it might explain a few things. Where the hell is this Claymont Drive anyway?"

"I already checked, Lieutenant. It's in a new subdivision east of Cahuenga, runs up toward the reservoir. And get this, Lieutenant, it's one helluva lot closer to Mulholland."

Brady was pulling on his jacket.

"Is Murphy still there?"

"I told him to wait."

Brady grabbed his .38 out of the desk drawer clipped it into the harness under his arm and jammed on his brown fedora. "Right," he said. "What are we waiting for. Let's get the hell out there and take a look."

Murphy was reading the racing pages when the squad car with Brady and Harrigan pulled up. He shoved the paper hurriedly under the seat, pulled on his cap and raised himself out of the patrol car.

"Sarge," he said, walking up as Brady and Harrigan emerged. "I took a good look around. Six twenty-one is unoccupied, as are all the others on this block."

"Unoccupied, all of them?" asked Harrigan.

"That's right, Sarge."

"Bloody peculiar."

Brady looked at Murphy. "You talk to anybody yet?"

"Just a woman a couple of blocks down, says she's seen people around here and thought they might be short term rentals. That's just her guess though."

"Right," said Brady. "Go back and see her and get a full statement, including the night in question, then carry on with your tour. Report to me personally when you get back to the station."

"Yes, sir."

Murphy got back into his car, turned it around, and drove off down the street. Brady and Harrigan stood for a moment looking around, then walked up the short drive of six twenty-one for a closer look. The house was a ranch-style Spanish, fairly new and looked well-maintained. There were wrought-iron grilles on the front windows, but the side ones had drapes, mostly closed, but through one they managed to see inside. The rooms were obviously furnished, albeit sparsely, but did not appear to have anything in the way of personal possessions. Just the way a rental might look.

"I'd say the lady down the block might be right," said Harrigan. "Should we get a warrant to search the place?"

"Not yet," said Brady. "First, I want to know who owns this place, and those others on the block. That will give us something to start with. At the moment there's not a damn thing to link Senna with this place. We may be completely off target."

Harrigan scribbled something down in his notebook.

They walked back and stood for a while on the concrete roadway by the car. Brady pulled his chin.

"How long do you reckon it would take to get to Mulholland from here?"

Harrigan reached into the Chevy and retrieved the Hollywood street map. "Depends on which way you go, but the shortest route would be to take Cahuenga to Hillpark Drive and you're there. No more than ten or twelve minutes."

Brady pushed his hat back on his head a little and chewed thoughtfully on a matchstick. "Okay, let's see. We got a slip of the tongue which could have brought Senna here that night. We got a location that fits a time frame from the murder to where the body was found. We also have the fact that a shot fired here would be very unlikely to be heard."

"Didn't the report say a silencer was used?"

"What it said Harrigan, was there was probablility one was used. Which means we have to consider both possibilities. What we still don't have though," he said half to himself, "is why."

Harrigan folded up the map and threw it through the window onto the back seat. "Just suppose for a moment, Lieutenant, this was where Senna was killed. His body was found in the trunk, so there must have been some blood around where the transfer took place."

Brady stuck some gum in his mouth and thought for a moment. "When did it last rain?" he said.

"Rain? Oh I see, not since the killing."

"Okay," said Brady. "Let's just suppose. If he was staking out this place, then it's a cinch he wouldn't be parked at the door, like we are. He'd have been back down the street someways. You take that side and I'll take this."

Harrigan crossed over and they both walked slowly down the street, eyes on the ground. About eighty yards along on the opposite side, Harrigan dropped down on one knee. "Lieutenant, there's something here."

Brady crossed over. "Looks like quite a few spots of something. Hey, there's a large one on the curb and another back here. Just about where the driver's door would have been."

"Looks like we just hit pay dirt, Lieutenant."

"Don't get too carried away, Harrigan. Could just be someone with a cut finger or a bloody nose. Anyway, get on the radio and get the forensic boys up here pronto."

Harrigan hurried back to the car. Brady sat on his haunches for a while staring at the ground. He shook his head slowly and swore softly under his breath. "What in hell's name did you see here, Tony, that managed to get half your head blown away."

13

Already several limousines lined the curb outside the Vermont on Sunset as the Yellow cab came to a halt. The driver pulled on the handbrake, turned around and looked over the seat.

"That'll be eighty-five cents," he said shifting a toothpick automatically from one side of his mouth to the other. "Looks like some swell crowd you're joining this evening, bud. You one of those movie stars?"

Frank gave a lean smile as he got out of the cab, took some bills from his pocket and peeled one off. "Now I wonder what gave you that impression," he said. He gave the cabbie a dollar even and strode off across the sidewalk.

The cabbie gave him a sour look. "Gee, I was just asking," he muttered to himself as he drove off. He much preferred picking up couples, the guys usually tipped high to impress the ladies.

The uniformed doorman glanced at Frank's pass, then touched his cap. Frank pushed through the swing doors of the hotel, and joined the stream of people headed for the mezzanine stair. A large hand-lettered sign indicated where the reception was being held.

Either side of the stair a couple of well-built studio security men were checking passes again. In spite of his low opinion of their worth, Ullrich was obviously taking no chances. What reason he had given them for requiring their presence Frank wasn't quite sure, but he noticed the tell-tale bulge under each of their arms that even a well-cut tuxedo couldn't hide. He had to admit their very presence might well deter anyone harbouring thoughts of murder.

As he checked through and walked up the short flight of stairs he could hear the band playing. He knew it wasn't, but it sounded a lot like Tommy Dorsey. At the open door of the suite a white-coated waiter stood with a tray of drinks. Frank accepted one and walked through. He stood for a moment and glanced around. The style of the place was heavily oriental. He fully expected to see Charlie Chan appear from behind a pillar at any moment.

Behind the band, which sat on a red-carpeted dais, hung a shimmering gold curtain with a huge dragon's head embroidered on it. A long way from the subject of the movie, perhaps that was the intention. Dining tables, unoccupied for the moment, were set loosely around a dance floor. Those guests who had arrived were clustered around the bar through an archway at the far end of the room.

Frank hesitated momentarily. The only face he recognised was Milton Feldman sporting another carnation in his buttonhole, who stood drinking on his own. Frank was trying to decide whether to join him when he felt two fingers prod him in the back.

"Howdy, pardner," said two voices in unison. He turned to see the grinning faces of Greenberg and Field.

"Well, if it isn't those two wonder boys from the writing department."

"Flattery will get you everywhere," grinned Bert.

"You fellas arrived right on cue. I was just trying to spot a friendly face."

"Don't worry your head about that, buddy," said Al. "That's one thing you can say about us. We are friendly faces."

Frank wondered if they'd still think that by the time this business was over.

"What's that you're drinking?" asked Bert.

"I haven't tried it yet. I picked it up at the door."

Bert whisked the glass out of his hand and set it on a nearby table. "My God don't drink that stuff, it's a local wine. Tastes like virgin's piss."

"Yeah," said Al. "We'll get the real thing at the bar."

Without further ado they propelled him across the

floor. Moments later, after some precise instructions to the bartender, all three were ensconced, each with a very dry Martini.

Frank glanced around the by now growing crowd. Feldman hovered nearby posing and trying to look important.

"Tell me something," asked Frank. "Why does that guy always wear a carnation?"

"Who, Feldman?"

"Yeah."

"That's because he's an ambitious little bastard who thinks he'll be running the studio in ten years," replied Al.

"Will he?"

"That little geek," said Bert. "He'll be lucky if he lasts out the year."

Frank wondered exactly how ambitious Feldman might be. Maybe he figured if Ullrich was out of the frame he'd be in line for the job. There were too many boy wonders around in this business not to think of it as a possibility, in spite of what Bert thought. Someone else for Ellie to check out.

He sipped some of his Martini and looked at the writers. "One thing that does surprise me, though, is why so many people attend these affairs."

"Are you kidding? Any chance to eat and drink at the studio's expense is welcomed with open arms, especially on our pay."

Frank put his glass down on the bar. "I gathered from

MULHOLLAND DRIVE

something Ullrich said that all you guys were pretty well paid."

"That's what he and the studio would like everyone to think, but don't you believe it, buddy," said Bert between gulps at his Martini.

"Mind you," added Al. "It's all right if your name is William Faulkner or Ben Hecht, then you can name your own price. But for us at the bottom of the totempole it's a different story."

"And since we don't like being bottom of the totempole" said Bert in turn, "we joined the Writers Guild. Although by the time they get round to getting us a raise, we'll probably have been fired anyway." He sighed, put his glass down on the bar and signaled for a refill.

Across the room some important looking studio executives had arrived. They were closely followed by the unmistakable figure of Ullrich, flanked by Lois and Linda, the film's publicist. In a moment they were surrounded by crowd of reporters and photographers.

The stars of the picture would not normally appear until later events or sometimes not until the premiere. Although, with the controversey surrounding this picture, maybe not even then.

After a few moments Lois detached herself from the group and crossed the room toward them. Most standing at the bar stopped their conversations to look.

She wore a long silvery grey dress with a high collar, slashed down one side like a cheong-sam. There was a glimpse of a perfect thigh. She carried a small bag that matched her Chinese red lipstick exactly. She looked absolutely stunning.

"Well I hope these two are not corrupting you," she said, looking at Frank.

"Too late for that, I'm afraid," he grinned. "Can I get you something to drink."

"Thanks. I'll have a gimlet."

As Frank turned to catch the bartender, Bert recovered his breath sufficiently to ask Lois. "What's a gimlet?"

"Well that really depends which part of the world you're in." She melted Bert's heart with a smile. "A real gimlet is two parts gin and one part Rose's Lime Juice, shaken and strained, then served on the rocks, but they don't always use the right juice. Beats a Martini hollow though. You should try it."

The bartender put a folded napkin on the bar and placed the pale greenish colored drink on it. The color matched the pale jade of her earrings.

She sipped her drink and looked across at Frank. "Well, since I'm to be your guide for the evening I'll have to detach you from the Katzenjammer Kids here and introduce you to the rest of the crew." She smiled at Bert and Al, and straightened Frank's bow tie with her free hand. For the second time that evening he was led across the floor. Al and Bert looked on with undisguised envy.

"You know," said Bert absently. "She does remind me

a little of someone."

"Who might that be? enquired Al.

"That's just it. I can't think."

Frank and Lois were halfway across the room. "That's a pretty sensational outfit you're wearing tonight," Frank said quietly. "That must have set you back a few bucks."

Lois laughed lightly. "I'll let you into a little secret. When I was organising your tux from the wardrobe department, I picked out a little something for myself. So we are both in borrowed clothes."

Frank grinned. "Now I know what it feels like to be an extra."

They stopped on the edge of a crowd surrounding Ullrich, at that moment the centre of attention. Lois gripped Frank's hand and looked at him, her face serious. "You think there's a chance anything might happen tonight?" she whispered.

"You mean to Ullrich?"

"Yes."

Frank shook his head. "I don't think so. I don't see our villain wanting to go out in a blaze of glory. I've no doubt, if he's here, he'll have seen the two security guards at the door. I think that might just be enough to deter him."

"Interesting that you said, he. Couldn't a woman be just as likely to have a motive?"

"I'm sure they could, but women tend to act more in the heat of the moment, rather than in a cold, premeditated way."

"Mmn," said Lois." You may be right."

Some time later after they'd eaten and Lois had disappeared to the powder room, Frank found himself standing next to Linda. Her eyes caught his. There was a tall glass in her hand with what looked like the remains of a Tom Collins.

"Well," she said. "Manage to get a good look at everyone?"

She spoke very carefully, like someone trying to show they hadn't had too much to drink. Frank looked back at her without any change in expression, seeing her close up for the first time. She was attractive in a hard sort of way, but her mouth was a little too wide and her lips a little too thin. She looked as if she'd heard most the opening lines and knew the answers to all of them. Her long dress in electric blue with wide shoulder straps and a low neckline showed an impressive cleavage. In that department she certainly wasn't lacking, although the rest of her figure was a little on the heavy side.

"I'm not sure I know what you mean," was his cool response.

"That sonofabitch Ullrich can't fool me. You're no more an adviser on the movie than the gateman."

Frank allowed himself a gentle smile. "I see. What led you to that conclusion?"

"Whose bed do you think he crawls back to when he's

finished playing with his latest starlet? No prizes for guessing. I knew about the letters a couple of weeks back, it wasn't until you appeared I figured he'd taken them seriously."

Although Frank was a little startled by the revelation regarding her sleeping arrangements, he wasn't sure how much she really knew or whether this was just her way of getting more information. He had no way of knowing of course if Ullrich had mentioned receiving the third letter. If he had to guess, he'd say no.

"That's very observant of you, Miss Salisbury, but you are well aware of the problems they've been having on the set, which could be a lot more serious than the odd crank letter."

She looked back at him as if trying to weigh up what he'd just said. She finished her drink without comment and put down the glass on a nearby table. There was a half smile on her face as she took a slim silver case from her purse and selected a cigarette.

"Smoke?" she offered.

"Not at the moment, thanks."

She fitted the cigarette into a small pearl holder and held it lightly between her fingers, waiting.

Frank produced his lighter. She took the light and looked him again in the eye.

"You look like a fairly smart guy, DeMarco, I'm sure you're not fooled by the tone of those letters." She blew some smoke in the air. "People with grudges can, and do, go to extraordinary lengths to taunt their victim, and be every bit as lethal as any mad dog killer."

"Oh yes, I'm well aware of that, Miss Salisbury. You do get to see the results of their efforts quite often in my line of work."

"I'm sure you do," she murmured. "I'm sure you do. No need to be quite so formal by the way, the name's Linda."

Frank sensed this was where the charm offensive would begin. He was wondering how to plan his escape when he saw Lois approaching.

"Frank," she said. "I'm sorry to have left you alone for so long, but I'm sure Linda has been looking after you."

She smiled sweetly.

Linda's eyes hardened for just a second. "We were just exchanging a little studio gossip. Now I really must be getting back to work. Publicity is a full time job."

He felt Lois take his arm. "Frank promised me a dance earlier this evening, so I'm going to hold him to it." She smiled again at Linda and guided him off toward the floor. The band was playing "Marie."

Frank paused for a moment. "How do you know I can dance?"

"It's easy, just put one foot in front of the other. You'll soon get the hang of it."

Frank smiled. "I'm sure I will. Who are the band by the way? They sound more like Dorsey than Dorsey."

"Just a crew from the studio. They specialize in sounding like anyone you want."

The singer, who sounded exactly like Jack Leonard

began, "Marie the dawn is breaking........"

"I might have guessed," said Frank. "After all, this is movietown - nothing is ever quite what it seems. Oh, and thanks for the timely rescue back there, by the way. A few more minutes and who knows."

Lois moved in a little closer. For the first time he caught the fragrance of her perfume. Whatever it was, it was expensive. "That's all right," she mur- mured, "all part of the service."

She gave him a running commentary on the few fresh faces they encountered on the floor, those she'd missed out on earlier in the evening.

When the music stopped she didn't release his arm.

"Well now, you didn't do to badly for your first lesson," she smiled.

"No, I guess not. I'm looking forward to the next one already."

Frank was finding the evening a good deal more entertaining than he expected, but he reminded himself that this was still work. He hadn't lost sight of Ullrich for more than a few moments during the evening, accepting that if someone were crazy enough to try anything there would be little he could do but pick up the pieces. But, as he'd said to Lois earlier, he didn't think something public was part of the gameplan.

After a while they drifted over to where Ullrich was posing for some photographs. Linda was naturally in close attendance.

"Well, fellows," Ullrich was saying, "I think you've all

got enough to make your editors happy. I have a busy day tomorrow, so I'll bid you gentlemen goodnight." He turned. "Ah, Frank, we're just about to leave, the car is out front now. Do you think you could see Lois to a cab?"

Frank nodded and glanced at Lois. Her face was enigmatic. They headed out through the double doors and down the steps to the hotel foyer, where Lois and Linda collected their wraps from the cloakroom. The two security men came forward to escort them out to the sidewalk, no doubt thankful the evening had passed uneventfully.

A cream-colored Cadillac sat by the curb, motor running. The uniformed doorman opened the car door and Linda and Ullrich got in quickly. Frank caught Linda's rather knowing glance as the Cadillac pulled out sharply into the late-night traffic on Sunset and sped off to the west.

He turned back to Lois, who seemed not to have noticed. "I can drop you off first if you like."

"Fine," she said.

He nodded to the doorman who raised his hand and signaled a Yellow cab from the rank.

14

Lois's apartment turned out be halfway along Laurel Avenue off Sunset in West Hollywood, no more than a ten minute ride. She was very quiet and held his arm most of the way.

The road was deserted as she signalled to the cabbie to stop and he pulled up under a pepper tree. She opened the door and stepped out.

"Won't you come in for a drink." she said casually, her hand on the open door. Frank hesitated, more for effect than anything else, because he knew this was one invitation he'd never be able to turn down.

"You're sure it's not too late?"

"Don't be silly this is Hollywood, and besides we're off duty now."

Frank paid off the cab driver who was obviously

trying to figure out which movie he might have seen her in. This time Frank was a little more generous with the tip.

Escorial Apartments was a newish apartment court built in the Spanish Colonial style and roofed in terracotta tiles. The name was etched in black script on the archway leading into the long courtyard. Overhead a pale moon hung low in the sky casting long hard shadows on the ground and turning the pink-flowered oleander bushes, lining the brick pathway, into pools of darkness.

They entered the lobby of Lois's building, passed the small concierge's office, empty now, and walked up the tiled stairs to the second floor. The walls were pale ivory paint over the rough plasterwork. A niche on the stair contained some sort of dried flower arrangement, at least that's what they looked like; maybe they were just dead.

The apartment itself was similar but the walls here were smooth and white, a large creamy rug covered the dark oak floor. Through the half-open door on the left he could see the cool whiteness of the bedroom. The main windows overlooked the central gardens. Few lights were showing from the apartments opposite: most people had retired by this time of night. Those lights that remained reflected in the waters of what Frank guessed was a small swimming pool.

Lois threw her bag on the chair, shrugged off her wrap, and went over to the drinks cabinet. "Make yourself at home," she said. "I'll mix the gimlets. And you can turn on the radio if you like, we might be able to get the real Tommy Dorsey."

Frank obliged, but kept it low, then sat down listening to the soft sounds of swing, and glanced around the room. The furnishings all had a certain newness about them. This was certainly one fancy apartment, he wondered vaguely how she could afford it. She'd be horrified if she ever saw his. Another, more persistent, thought began to force its way into his mind, perhaps she wasn't paying her own rent. That was something he really didn't want to think about.

"Penny for your thoughts." She was standing beside him with two drinks in her hands.

"I was just thinking how nice an apartment you have here."

"Well, I do share it with a girl friend," she replied without a moment's hesitation. "She's away at the moment."

It came so quickly off her tongue that Frank pushed any lingering doubts from his mind. He relaxed, smiled, and sipped his drink. "By the way where did you get your taste for gimlets?" he asked, making conversation.

"Oh here and there," she said. "It's originally an English drink you know, well the lime juice part of it anyway. All those hot colonial outposts of empire."

"Tastes great just the same."

Lois smiled lazily. "What did you think of our lady publicist?"

"About the same way as I think of a piranha."

Lois's smile broadened. "Well, they do say she's looking for her third husband."

She moved down on to the davenport beside him, crossing a long, nylon-sheathed leg in the process. The split in the dress fell away exposing a curve of elegant thigh. She seemed not to have noticed.

She tasted her drink, her eyes larger when she looked up. "You saw everyone connected with the picture tonight. Any idea who our note sender might be?"

"Which one?"

"You mean you think there's two?" There was a hint of surprise in her voice.

"Oh yes, I'm fairly certain of that."

"What makes you so sure or shouldn't I ask?"

Frank placed his empty glass carefully on the small side table and smiled. "No reason why not, we're both on the same team, aren't we?"

Her lips were slightly parted, moist and very red, and suddenly seemed very close to his. "So we are," she murmured. "So we are."

The symmetry of her face was perfect, her skin lightly tanned. He wondered what the rest of her body might be like. "Well, it really all comes down in the end to sophistication," he said. "Unless, of course, we're dealing with some criminal mastermind. Which I doubt."

"Sophistication?" Her eyes widened.

"Yes, you know, education, culture, refinement."

She was so close he caught again the fragrance of her perfume and the rich scent of her golden hair.

She looked at him, her eyes lucid.

"Makes sense I suppose," she breathed. "Does this make sense?"

Her partly open mouth gently brushed his several times before he tasted the soft warmth of those Chinese red lips.

She fell into his arms.

Frank opened his eyes, Lois's soft mane of blonde hair lay spread on the pillow beside him. Bright moonlight streamed through the window casting squares of silver light on the counterpane. In a shadow by the bed a small luminous clock glowed. 1.25am.

He turned and watched the gentle rise and fall of her breast as she slept. Easing himself out of bed he began to dress. His golden rule was never to wake up in someone else's bed. Better the dream than the reality of the morning after.

He stood for a moment as he finished dressing and looked out the window. The moonlight was casting long, deep shadows across the courtyard, touching the trees with a cold, silvery light. The apartments opposite were in total darkness. For a second he thought he caught a movement by the edge of the pool, but when he looked back there was nothing.

As he noted down Lois's telephone number off the phone by the bed he glanced at a framed photograph showing two girls posing in front of a large house. One was obviously Lois, the other, also very attractive, looked younger. Probably a friend, he thought. He left the room quietly and slipped out of the apartment thinking an early morning telephone call might catch her before she awoke.

A light wind rustled through the leaves as he emerged from under the dark shadow of the pepper trees and headed down Laurel, turning up the collar of his tuxedo against the chill. The bright lights of the boulevard glowed in the distance. He had no doubt he'd be able to pick up a cab.

Thoughts of Lois came back to him and he could visualize her as she lay on the counterpane. He could still feel the warmth of that body against his and the taste of those soft red lips. Her perfume was an indelible memory.

About a hundred yards back up the road the dark shape of a Plymouth sedan, the engine note faint, detached itself from the long, black shadows and began to edge forward.

Slowly at first, then closer and closer, it came.

What sixth sense alerted Frank he would never know, but for some reason he glanced over his shoulder.

The Plymouth had one tire on the sidewalk, the driver a hunched dark shape at the wheel. At that moment the driver gunned the engine. Without a second thought Frank threw himself over the low wall of an apartment house just as the sedan scrapped its fender along the stonework inches from his leg.

The ridiculous thought went through his head as to how he would explain the state of the tuxedo when he returned it to wardrobe department on Monday. Landing in some shrubs on the other side of the wall Frank caught a glimpse of green paintwork as the sedan sped off toward the boulevard. With brake lights glowing red and tires squealing it skidded around the corner and vanished.

15

It was a few minutes after eleven the following Monday morning when the phone in Jack Warner's outer office began to ring. It was Bill Schaefer, his personal aide, who answered it.

"Yes. Who?...L.B. Hold on a moment, I'll try and connect you."

He buzzed J.L.'s line several times but got no answer. Bill muttered to himself as he got up, crossed the room and opened the office door. There was no-one in the room, but the door to the executive bathroom was ajar.

"Mr Warner?" he called.

"Yes?" came a muffled reply.

"Telephone for you."

"I'm on the john. Who is it?"

"It's L.B. Mayer."

There was silence for a moment.

"Tell him I'll call him right back. I can only deal with one shit at a time."

Jack Warner was loud, brash and the archetypal Hollywood mogul, with slicked-back hair and a pencil-thin moustache. Jack was also master of all he surveyed. "Would all that be there," he is reputed to have said, pointing at the humming activity of the studio, "if I didn't know what the fuck I was doing?"

Jack knew that basically he was running a factory and like any other kind of factory it required discipline and order. The only difference was, this factory produced movies.

Ten minutes later he was back at his desk and reconnected to L.B. Mayer at MGM studios.

"How are you L.B.? Sorry I was otherwise engaged for a moment."

"That's alright, Jack. I got the *Hollywood Reporter* in front of me here. They say you're going ahead with the release of that anti-Nazi movie you've been talking about."

"That's right L.B."

"Don't you think you ought to give this a little more thought? I mean this could do us a lot of harm."

Jack rolled an unlit cigar between his fingers.

"With whom, L.B.?"

"Look, Jack, a lot of us are still booking pictures in Germany and taking money out of there. We're not at war with Germany, nobody is yet, and you're going to hurt some of our own people."

"Hurt what, L.B.? Their pocketbooks? Listen, those murdering bastards killed our man Joe Kaufman in Germany because he wouldn't heil Hitler. The Silver Shirts and the Bundists and all the rest of these hoods are marching in Los Angeles and New York right now. There are high school kids with swastikas on their sleeves a few blocks from our studio. Is that what you want in exchange for some crummy royalties out of Germany?"

At the other end of the phone L.B. had gone as white as the celebrated decor of his Cedric Gibbon- designed office.

He spluttered. "Jack, that isn't what I meant and you know it. All I'm saying is we need to be very careful. There are still lots of our own people back there. Think about how they could be hurt."

"It is them I'm thinking about, L.B. Somebody has got to tell America what those bastards are really up to over there. Now, I don't want to mention any names, but some very important people in Washington want this movie made. There's gonna be a fucking war. You know it and I know it, and before long we'll all be up to our god-damn necks in it."

"Okay, okay," said L.B., a note of resignation in his voice. He knew better than to argue when Jack was in this mood. "Really, in my heart, I know you're right. All I would say is, watch out, these guys play for keeps."

Jack sat for a long time after he had finished the call

before he finally lit the cigar. To him good headlines made good movies, at least that was what he was always telling his writers.

In this case the previous year a Nazi spy ring had been rounded up in New York by the FBI and the participants convicted of espionage. The full story had been told in the *New York Post* in a dramatic series of articles entitled 'Storm over America' by Leon Turrou, the agent in charge. Jack had not needed much prompting to consider a movie, especially after his man in Germany had been murdered and Ullrich had approached him with the idea. Although he had to think hard about the obvious risk to the studio and its employees. He also knew about the letter Ullrich had just received and that things would be very unlikely to end there.

None of this, of course, he'd mentioned to L.B. The question was, how much further would these people go? Maybe, if he was any good, this private eye Ullrich hired would find out. At some point it might be wise to go public, preferably when the movie was ready for release. After all, you couldn't buy that sort of publicity. Jack always had an eye for the main chance.

The red warning light above the entrance to sound stage eight blinked off and the burly uniformed guard stood aside to let Frank enter. He stepped from bright morning sunshine into an alien world of semi-darkness lit here and there by pools of brightness. There was a buzz of activity as the crew prepared to move to the next set for a new scene.

All around were props of all descriptions and the floor was a maze of wires and cables. To Frank it looked like barely controlled chaos. The sets at this end of the huge, cavernous building looked like those for this movie. But beyond were a number of others. At the far end he could see what looked like a full size mock up of a Spanish galleon. Two years hence this stage would be the scene of one of Warners' greatest movies, *Casablanca,* but at this moment in time it was only a half-written play.

Off to one side the actors stood in a group, each studying a script in preparation for the next take. They were the only ones Frank had not had a chance to observe since none had attended the reception in the Vermont. He studied the cast list that Lois had given him. It showed each actor and the part he was playing in the movie, along with a few notes about the character.

Neville Beaumont was the lean, smooth, sophisticated type. As an Englishman he was naturally cast as a Nazi spy, although at this point in the movie he had yet to be unmasked. Along with Edward G Robinson and Francis Lederer he was rehearsing the next scene.

Frank hovered in the background for a moment and studied them. It was hard to imagine any of them being involved in a plot to disrupt the movie. He glanced around the soundstage. It was positively labyrinthian. If anyone was intent on sabotage, the opportunities were endless. Frank found a vacant canvas chair and sat down to watch.

The director was striding about issuing a stream of directions. Both writers had their heads together discussing something. He spotted Milton Feldman but of Ullrich, however, there was no sign. Frank checked his watch, it was well after eleven-thirty. Perhaps he'd been detained somewhere.

The case was beginning to take on a familiar profile, the threats, the sabotage and the attempt to kill him. He had no doubt, after Friday night, that that had been the object. A fact which on the face of it seemed rather curious, something the opposition might be tempted to do if they thought he was getting too close. So far he didn't have a single suspect, but perhaps they were unaware of that and simply felt his presence constituted a danger. He'd only caught a fleeting glimpse of the car in the darkness, but he had no doubt it was the one that had been tailing him all week. Maybe he was closer than he realised.

Captain Malone eyed Brady and Harrigan in turn, but did not invite either to sit down.

"Since we don't appear to have an arrest on this case, Lieutenant, I trust we have some very convincing reasons why not."

Brady glanced quickly at the other man in the room. He was sitting alongside the desk and Malone had not bothered to introduce him. He recognised Carmady, the new assistant DA.

Brady laid the Senna file deliberately on the desk. At the end of the interview if the Captain picked it up, Brady would know he was very definitely off the case. "We now have a complete picture of events leading up to the murder, including the location where it was carried out."

Malone's face didn't change. "Go on, Phil," was all he said.

"On the Friday before his death Tony Senna spent the entire day at the track in Hollywood Park. We have a number of witnesses who will attest to that. On his return that evening he was given the address of the following night's stakeout by the night man at his apartment block. This was the address where the couple in the case were supposed to be meeting."

"Who left this address?"

"Benny Walsh, an occasional gofer for both Senna and DeMarco."

"You have proof of that?" interjected Carmady.

"Yes, sir. We have a statement from Walsh plus confimation from both men at the apartment block."

"Both?" snapped Malone.

"Yes, the original message was left with the day man, but by the time his shift ended at six Senna had not returned, so he passed it to the night man."

"Carry on."

"This is the critical turning point of the whole case,

because one or both of these men got the address wrong. Instead of 621 Braemont it became 621 Claymont."

"Didn't either of them write it down?"

"They both said they did. They take messages all the time, but they're just scribbled on a pad and thrown away at the end of the shift. Neither could swear which address was correct, so either one could have made the error. But we do have Walsh's testimony as to which he gave over the telephone in the first place."

Malone's face was inscrutable, but Carmady was leaning forward with interest.

"Senna had no reason to suspect anything was wrong," Brady continued. "Even if he had, there was no way he could check."

"Why was that?" asked Carmady.

"Walsh had already left for San Francisco."

"Does that check out?"

"It does. Our last confirmed sighting of Senna that Saturday night was at an Italian restaurant on Sunset. From there, we surmise, he went directly to 621 Claymont to stakeout the wrong property. Sometime later that evening, around midnight, he was shot to death at close range from behind with a .38, possibly silenced, weapon."

Carmady spoke again. "Proof?"

Brady opened the file and passed Carmady the forensic report. "There's a photograph of the slug, recovered from the vehicle, and traces of blood were found on the sidewalk at the scene, a perfect match with Senna's. We are certain that's where he was killed, and where the body was transferred to the trunk."

Carmady examined the photograph. "The slug looks pretty mashed up, they sure it's a .38?"

"Near as they can tell, Mr Carmady."

"What I'm more interested in," said Malone, interrupting tonelessly. "Is by whom."

Brady smiled faintly. "At this point person or persons unknown."

Carmady lit a thin cigar and looked across at Brady. "What about this partner of his? Wasn't he supposed to be a suspect?"

"Not in my book, never has been." Brady looked directly at Malone as he said it. "But if there had been any doubt, now we have irrefutable proof. Even if DeMarco had somehow learned the address of the stakeout, he could never have known that Senna would be given a different one or what it would be."

Carmady nodded sagely. "There is, of course, another possibility," he mused. "Senna could have phoned DeMarco himself and told him the location. Is that not so, Lieutenant?"

"That is a possibility," admitted Brady. "But..."

"Damn right it's a possibility," butted in Malone.

Brady knew he was on very thin ice here, but sensed Carmady was the man who would make the ultimate decision on whether they pursued this line of enquiry or dropped it.

"Either way," said Brady, ignoring Malone, "there's absolutely no evidence to suggest it. But let's assume for a moment he did make a call. We have definite sightings of DeMarco at the Delmar club from when he arrived at nine until he left at around twelve-thirty. We know he took no calls while he was there, because we checked. So any call would have had to have been made earlier."

"So what's your point, Lieutenant?"

"The point is, regardless of whether he knew or not, it would have taken him at least an hour to get to Claymont Drive and back, never mind the trip to Mulholland. Had he been absent for that length of time then it would have been noticed."

Malone's face was inscrutable, but Carmady nodded in agreement. "A while back you said persons. How do you figure that?" he asked.

"Well, after the killing someone had to drive Senna's car to the spot on Mulholland where it was found. That person would have had no way of getting back unless another car had followed. Something else that lets DeMarco off the hook."

"Of course, of course," said Carmady. "Have you any idea what might actually have happened?"

"Well, apparently six twenty-one and several of the surrounding properties are used as rental units. None, however, are presently occupied. We thought someone could have been using them as meeting place or a hideout, but that's improbable since there were no signs of forced entry. Whatever, Senna was just in the wrong place at the wrong time. On the other hand, if it had been a hit, he could have been followed and someone saw their opportunity when he parked."

"Any witnessess at the scene?"

"The nearest was a woman who lives two blocks down, all she can recall is hearing some cars late that night. She was in bed and didn't get up to look."

"Have you checked if there's a tie-in with any other current cases?" asked Malone.

"We have, but nothing connects."

"And did you, Phil," went on Malone coldly, "in all this toing and froing, find out who owns this god-damn house?"

Brady closed the file which had remained open since he'd removed the forensic report and squared it neatly on the desktop. "We did."

"We're waiting, Lieutenant."

"Warner Brothers Studios."

16

The crisp California sun sparkled off the rooftops of the cars in the studio parking lot as Frank pulled out and drove toward the gate. The gateman, whose name he had discovered was Owens, gave him a cheery wave as he passed through. Such people never knew whether today's nobody may turn into tomorrow's star, so it always paid to be deferential.

He turned the black La Salle roadster onto Barham Boulevard with a curious sense of detachment and unreality. Only ten minutes earlier he had returned to his small office in the writers' building after watching that morning's filming on stage eight. Since Ullrich had not shown up, he had checked with Lois to check if he was in his office. Her first words were that she thought he'd been on the set. Frank had waited while she checked around the studio before trying Ullrich's home number. There'd been no reply. Probably nothing, she thought, but still she agreed he should go and check. She was quite sure there'd be some innocent explanation. He'd scribbled down the address on the back of one of his business cards.

1658 Hillcrest in Beverly Hills.

As he drove, Frank's thoughts were mostly about Lois. She had still been asleep when he'd called on the Saturday morning, but they had met later for lunch and spent the rest of the weekend together. Frank was a realist, however, and never let his personal life get in the way of a case. He took what came his way and didn't complain if that was all there was.

Right now Karl Ullrich was his concern, although he didn't see much point in jumping to any conclusions just yet. Frank pushed the speed limit all he dared, but this was daytime, the traffic was heavier and the occasional speedcop was in evidence.

Los Angeles was a big city and had grown a great deal faster than anyone had planned. Of course they could always blame William Mulholland for that. At present it covered around 400 odd square miles of loosely connected suburbs. Hollywood itself having a certain Baroque charm. Beverly Hills, formerly called the Land of the Gathering Waters, was another suburb, but the only things that gathered now were the rich and famous to build their status symbol homes.

It was after one when he picked up Hillcrest Drive

MULHOLLAND DRIVE

off Sunset. He slowed to a crawl looking for the number. House after house went by, their wide, emerald green lawns receiving constant attention from Japanese gardeners. As Goldwyn, might have said if Mullholland had been alive today he'd be spinning in his grave.

The house was big and white, one of those streamlined Moderne places, all rounded corners and glass block with horizontal windows and flat roofs. A style inspired by the current American love affair with machines, which had changed the shape of virtually everything from trains to toasters. It was the new machine art. Honest, simple and above all functional.

Not that Frank was someone who took all that much interest in design, but if you lived in Hollywood you ought not to be surprised by anything. He hadn't thought of Ullrich as having any particular taste one way or the other, but he must have pulled off a pretty sweet deal with Warners to afford a place like this. Of course he might be investing Ullrich with taste he didn't have, the place might just be a rental.

Frank pulled the La Salle into the horseshoe driveway and parked. There were no other cars in sight and the garage doors were closed. He walked up the short flight of steps, paused in front of the jade green door, and pressed the bell.

He heard it ring faintly inside.

Some moments went by.

No one answered.

He glanced idly around. The entrance was well screened from the road by a tall hedge and trees grew all around. The neighbourhood seemed quiet, some birds chattering in the trees and the occasional splash from a nearby swimming pool were the only sounds that drifted in the warm air. Just about what you might expect on a sunny Monday in early March, at least for those who hadn't a care in the world.

He tried the door, but to no avail, then decided to check the rear. The first thing he noticed was the venetian blinds on the front windows. They were still in the closed position. That was rather curious. Was it possible that Ullrich had spent the weekend at Linda's place and not returned home on Friday after the reception? Come to think of it he hadn't seen Linda at the studio that morning either. Perhaps they'd gone off somewhere together? Odd though without telling anyone. He was beginning to think he should have checked a little more before coming out. Ullrich would probably turn up at the studio, wondering what all the fuss was about.

As he came around the back he saw a large rectangular swimming pool set below the terrace. The inviting aquamarine water sparkled lazily in the afternoon sun. There were some striped blue loungers around the pool, but there was no-one in them. If Ullrich had a Japanese gardener then this must be his day off.

To his left was a long porch broken by a pair of

French windows. Again the blinds were closed. Frank hesitated for a moment, then reached out and tried one of the handles. The chrome lever clicked softly under his hand and the door swung silently inward. A wave of cool air swept over him, but there was a hint of something else.

"Hullo?" he called.

He stood for a moment tense and alert, not moving.

There was no reply. Again the house was absolutely still. Before he stepped onto the pale, buttery oak parquet floor Frank sensed what he was going to find.

His eyes took a few moments getting accustomed to the dimness of the room. It was obviously a study. A large grey rug covered most of the floor. There was a walnut bureau full of various cups and trophies, a wall of framed photographs, and a couple of cantilever chairs in tan leather arranged either side of a shiny black and chrome desk.

It wasn't any of these things that claimed Frank's attention, however, but the elegantly shod foot that stuck out grotesquely from underneath the desk.

Ullrich wasn't going to be enjoying any more sweet deals or indulging whatever taste he had for design, now or ever. He was obviously very, very dead.

Frank walked around behind the swivel chair, careful not to disturb anything. Ullrich had been shot in the chest from close range, the front of his argyle sweater a congealed mess. No matter how important you were in Hollywood, you couldn't argue with a piece of lead.

At some point the body had slipped down between the chair and the desk. A considerable amount of blood had run out of him, most of which had soaked into the grey carpet leaving a large black-looking stain.

He did a quick scan of the desk. There was the usual array of odds and ends including an onyx pen set with a matching ashtray which held the remains of a burnt out cigar. On the big leather-edged blotter lay a copy of the shooting script for the movie, splashed now with drops of dried blood. To one side, along with a half drunk glass of scotch, were a number of personal photographs in silver frames. Most appeared to be of women. One frame, however, was conspicuously empty.

Frank looked a little closer at the body. From the size of the wound it looked like a single shot had been fired at fairly close range. He could only guess, but it looked like he was killed sometime late last night, judging from the condition of the body, although the air-conditioning would have slowed things down a little there.

He stood still for several minutes his mind whirling with the implications. The notes, the movie, and where this left him. He glanced around the room. Nothing else seemed out of place, there was no sign of a disturbance or any sort of struggle. Ullrich must have known his killer and been talking to him to allow him to get this close. Of course he could also have been walked in from the front door at gunpoint, so that didn't tell him anything.

There were a lot of questions to be asked, but they

would have to wait. He checked his watch again, more than ten minutes had passed since his arrival.

He went out into the hall to look for a telephone.

"Yeah, Homicide please, Lieutenant Brady."

A voice came over the wire. "Hullo?" it said.

"Phil?"

"Yeah. Who is this?"

"It's Frank. I'm in Beverly Hills. There's a guy here I just came to check on. He's been shot."

"Is he dead?"

"Extremely, Phil. "

"Murdered?"

"No question. One in the chest, sometime last night I'd guess."

"What's the address?"

"1658 Hillcrest. Phone, Crestview 542."

"Okay, Frank. Sit tight, you know the drill. And don't touch a thing," he emphasised. "We'll be right out."

Frank put the receiver back down thoughtfully, then lit a cigarette. From where he sat by the hall table he could see through into the all white lounge. It looked like an RKO set for a Fred Astaire movie.

After a little while he called Lois.

The drive was crowded with police cars. It looked like Brady had brought half the Homicide division with him.

Brady spent several minutes on his haunches looking at the body, then waved to the photographic boys and the fingerprint men to get busy. He turned to Frank.

"Okay, you better give me chapter and verse."

Frank gave him a brief run-down of the morning's events right up to the moment of his call.

"That's all?"

"Depends what you mean by all."

Brady rolled his eyes. "Let's not get into that shit again, Frank. This guy was your client, right?"

Frank shook out a cigarette and lit it. There weren't that many honest cops on the force, but he knew Brady was one of them.

"He was."

"What were you working on?"

"That's client attorney privilege, Phil."

"Not if it involves the motive for his death," said Brady curtly. "Does it?"

Frank shrugged. "That's impossible to say at this stage, but there have been threats at the studio against both him and the movie."

"What fucking movie?"

"It was released to the press at the week-end. 'Storm Over America'. An anti-Nazi movie."

"Shit. Not that can of worms." Brady groaned.

"Sorry, Phil. Looks like you got yourself some Bund members to chase. Can I go now?"

"Definitely not. You'll come downtown and make a full statement. I've only just got Malone off my back on the Senna case and I don't want him back on it over this one."

Frank knew better than to ask about Tony at the moment. Brady would tell him in his own good time. Sergeant Harrigan appeared at his elbow.

"Medical examiner reckons time of death between ten and midnight judging from the condition of the body and allowing for the fact the room temperature was down low. Looks like a single shot from a small calibre gun, probably a .32, anything bigger would have made a lot more mess. No shell casing though. Our killer must have taken them with him."

Frank glanced across at the mess of blood on the floor. "Looks like the only bit of housekeeping he did."

"Still cracking wise, Frank." said Brady dryly. "Do you really think this is the work of our Bundist friends?"

"That's hard to say, Phil. I wouldn't rule out something personal though, there's a lot of crazy people in Hollywood. One thing though, it sure as hell wasn't robbery."

Harrigan frowned. "How do you know that?"

"Well, if I'm not mistaken, the picture over there on the wall is a Renoir. Any burglar could retire on the proceeds of that alone."

Brady could see the next question forming in Harrigan's mind, like who was this guy Renoir? So he grabbed Frank's arm and spoke first. "Harrigan just you make sure the lab boys dust everything on the desk for prints. Okay, Frank, let's go. Malone will enjoy seeing your ugly mug downtown even if it is only for a statement."

Frank was about to protest, but he realised it would be futile.

As they moved toward the front door, Brady stopped and turned. "By the way Frank, you carrying?"

"I am."

"Better let me check. Just for the record."

Frank unclipped the snub-nosed .38 Chief's Special from the rig under his jacket and handed it over butt first.

Brady put the barrel to his nose.

"Seems okay. Where do you keep your shells?"

"Loose in my pocket, Phil, just in case."

"Hmmph," was all he replied.

Outside Brady managed to extricate his car from the traffic jam on the drive and drove in silence until they made the turn onto Sunset.

"Ain't you gonna ask about Tony?" he said finally.

"I figured you'd tell me when you were ready, Phil," observed Frank quietly.

"Well, we don't have a killer just yet, but we're getting closer, at least we know exactly where the killing took place."

Frank sat up in his seat. "Where?"

"Certainly not the address Benny got for him, that's for sure. The night man gave it out wrong. "You still didn't say where."

"Six twenty-one Claymont, east of Cahuenga."

"How the hell...."

Brady looked across at him as he went straight ahead

on Holloway toward Santa Monica Boulevard.

"Just a slip of the tongue Frank, a goddamn slip of the tongue. Braemont became Claymont and somebody died."

"How can you be sure?"

"Traces of blood on the sidewalk. A match. But that's not all, Frank. We checked out who owns six twenty-one."

"And who might that be?"

"Some recent friends of yours I believe. The Brothers Warner."

Frank sat very still for some time. They cruised on quietly through the afternoon traffic before re-joining Sunset for the long drop downtown.

"Hey," said Frank. "You just ran a light."

Brady grinned lopsidedly. "Cops get to have some fun too you know."

17

The tallest building in Los Angeles was the dramatic, 28-story, gleaming white tower of City Hall, completed in 1928 in the Art Deco style. Clad in limestone, it had a Mayan style roof stepped like a pyramid and many other fine architectural features. It also housed the Homicide Bureau.

They left Frank, armed only with a pack of Lucky Strike, sitting in an interrogation room on the ninth floor for a full twenty minutes before anyone appeared. Apart from Lt Brady there was a female stenographer, Carmady, the new assistant DA, and last, but definitely not least, Captain Malone. He and Carmady took the two chairs opposite Frank, with the stenographer at a small table behind. Brady was left standing.

"Well, now," said Malone unable to keep the oily

smile off his face. "Look who we have here, our old friend, Mr DeMarco. Looks like you've been a little careless, Frank, losing a client like that. That is, of course, unless you and he had some sort of falling out, and you bumped him off yourself."

Frank knew better than to show any reaction, which was precisely what Malone was after. He drew quietly on his cigarette and waited.

Seeing his words had no effect, Malone's voice hardened. "Now, just give us the facts leading up to this murder, and how you came to be involved in it. And don't leave any fucking thing out."

Frank wondered if the stenographer was trained to leave out the expletives or edit them out afterwards. He looked across at Malone and was immediately reminded of all the reasons why he disliked the man. He wore a sweat stained, white shirt with the top button undone. A grubby brown tie hung slackly under his chin. His face displayed a self-satisfied smirk. It amazed Frank how guys like this ever made it to the top. Perhaps it was something the job itself turned them into.

Frank had already decided to tell everything that was in the public domain. They'd learn it eventually when they questioned the crew at the studio. Which also meant that they would unwittingly confirm his cover story for being there in the first place. Anything purely between himself and Ullrich was another matter however, and one he intended to keep to himself for the moment. As was Friday night's attempt on his life.

Everyone remained silent as he related the events, starting with his meeting with Ullrich in the Brown Derby. The only person working was the stenographer.

"Let me get this straight," said Malone, when he'd finished, his small, cruel eyes narrowing. "This guy hired you to advise them on the movie and at the same time look into some incidents on the set that may have been sabotage."

"Right," said Frank.

"Then last week this letter arrives with a specific threat saying that if the movie was to appear Ullrich wouldn't be around to see it?"

"That's correct."

"Bullshit, DeMarco! If that was the threat, why the hell kill him now? According to what you've said the movie is still in production, and they ain't had no chance so far to stop it."

Frank was well aware of the contradiction, but he didn't know the answer either. "That isn't my problem, Captain." he said lighting another cigarette. "I told you about the part I played in the events. Nothing more. I wasn't offering you the solution."

Malone's eyes were ice-hard. "Cute, DeMarco, very cute. This letter you referred to," he said through gritted teeth. "Where is it now?"

"At the studio, I assume, in Ullrich's office."

"And I suppose you have a very convincing reason why you didn't report it to the police?"

"Well, for one thing it wasn't my call. Ullrich decided there was no immediate threat and he was safe at least until the film came out, so he decided to carry on regardless."

Malone's mouth twisted "He sure as fuck doesn't think that now, does he?"

Frank kept his face expressionless, his eyes carrying their own thoughts. A narrow ribbon of smoke drifted upward from the end of his cigarette.

Carmady, a silver-haired man in his early fifties, leaned forward and rested his elbows carefully on the desk, concerned no doubt for his expensive suit.

"Mr DeMarco," he said, placing his fingertips together. "Can I ask you who you think may be responsible for this so-called sabotage on the set?"

Frank stroked his chin. "We don't know that yet. It follows it has to be someone working at the studio, but that could mean any one of hundreds of extras or hired hands."

"I see....What sort of thing are we talking about?"

"The most serious was an arc light which fell about twenty feet. The screws had been loosened and when the boom was moved it fell. Otherwise mostly small things apparently, like moving things on the set which aren't noticed until the filming's done, so it doesn't match the previous day's work and has to be re-shot. It all adds up to a lot of expense and delay."

"I see," said Carmady. "Do you think some of these people might be Nazi sympathizers?"

"That would seem like a fair bet. There's nothing to stop any one of these people hurrying home, slipping on their armbands and attending the nearest Bund meeting, now is there?"

"That's true, Mr DeMarco, that's true. But a little sabotage and disruption is still a long way from putting a .32 slug into someone's chest, is it not?"

Frank shrugged again. "As I understand it, some of these people are fanatics, but your guess is as good as mine."

"Okay, okay," said Malone impatiently. He could see they were getting nowhere fast. "That about wraps this up." He signalled to the stenographer to finish, then looked back at Frank. "Lieutenant Brady will accompany you out to Warner Studios in the morning so we can verify your version of events."

Frank kept his face expressionless. "Does that mean I can go?"

Malone tilted his chair back and narrowed his eyes. "What it means, DeMarco, is you'll be our guest for the night. I don't want you running off talking to anybody before we can confirm your story."

Frank's eyes turned to the assistant DA. "Can he do that?"

Carmady smiled and shrugged.

Malone gave a lopsided grin. "Well we can always book you on suspicion, if you'd rather and then find out our mistake next week."

"Okay, okay." Frank knew when he was hooked. "Can

I at least make a telephone call? I did have some plans for tonight."

Malone leered and looked as if he was about to take great delight in saying no, but Carmady gave a slight nod of his head.

"Okay," said Malone reluctantly. "So long as Lieutenant Brady listens to every word."

18

Next morning the black banner headlines on all the newsstands screamed the news:

WARNER MOVIE PRODUCER
SHOT TO DEATH IN BEVERLY HILLS

In the City jail reception on Temple Street Frank was seated reading those same headlines. The story was a little short on detail and no mention had been made of any connection with the movie. Frank was sure it wouldn't take them long to get around to that. The police statement merely confirmed they were treating it as murder and a full investigation was under way. They weren't giving much away, but it wouldn't be long before those newshounds started digging into Ullrich's past to see if any skeletons appeared. They were were nothing if not diligent.

Frank tossed the paper onto the bench as Brady walked into the room.

"Have a comfortable night, Frank?"

"About as good as one can in the circumstances. What do they fill those mattresses with, broken rocks?"

Brady gave a crooked smile. "Can't say I've tried them myself. By the way I had your car brought in last night from the scene by one of the uniform men. It's in the car park. I'll just sign you out, then drop you over there." Brady scribbled his signature as the desk sergeant pushed Frank's .38 across the counter. "I guess you'll be needing this too."

"Thanks, Phil." He slid the gun back under his arm and grinned. If they'd been a little more thorough they might have found the throwing knife he kept strapped to his forearm. "Do you need me right away at the studio? I'd like to go and get cleaned up a little."

Brady pulled his chin. "I don't think Malone would like it, but I guess it'll be okay. You gave a statement, that should be enough. Of course if anything comes up we need to check...."

"Don't worry, Phil, I'll be out by mid-morning."

Frank had plenty of time to think about events during his night in the cells. He was forced to agree with Malone's first reaction that this whole thing didn't seem to add up. It was all too easy to see plots around every corner, but somehow he knew there was a lot more to come in this case.

He'd also had time to think about Tony. Two weeks had passed since the murder. It was always a mistake to think that because you were inactive on a case meant that nothing was happening. Things have a habit of happening, all on their own.

Brady's revelation that Tony had been murdered outside a house belonging to Warners had been startling to say the least. Whether it was anything other than bizarre coincidence remained to be seen.

As soon as he got into his apartment he put in a call to Lois at the studio, told her the cops were on their way and gave her some precise instructions. Then he showered and shaved, put on a clean shirt and made himself a cup of coffee. Next stop would have to be the office, or Ellie would be thinking he'd taken up permanent residence at the studio.

The ride across town was anything but normal. After stopping at Schwab's counter for eggs on toast and more coffee, he was turning onto Sunset when he spotted another tail. This time it was the brown, late model Chevy. You had to hand it to them, these guys were nothing if not persistent.

Frank figured the time had come for a showdown. He got into the inside lane as he waited for the light on Western, then took a sharp right. Down a couple of blocks there was a parking garage with an exit onto an alley at the rear. Two minutes later, after weaving through, he cut back onto Western and parked behind a grey sedan three cars back from his pursuers. They'd pulled into the curb near the entrance, presumably waiting for him to emerge on foot.

Frank edged up on the street side and whipped open the rear door. He was in the back seat of the Chevy, with his .38 Smith and Wesson Chief's Special in the driver's neck, before either man had time to turn round.

"Okay fellas, just relax and keep your hands where I can see them. And no sudden moves. I didn't get all my beauty sleep last night, so I'm not in all that good a mood."

"You're making a big mistake, pal...." said the man in the passenger seat without turning round.

Frank cut him off. "We'll see who's making the mistake. Now you can start by telling me who you are and why you're following me. Your answers had better be good. Very good."

"Like I was about to say, you're making a big mistake. Now, how's this for being very good? We're agents of the Federal Bureau of Investigation."

Frank blinked. This definitely wasn't in the script.

"Oh, is that so," he said acidly. "I wasn't aware that the FBI went around following people then trying a hit and run."

The driver turned around quickly, his face reddening, the short barrel of the blue steel .38 Special ending up near his adam's apple.

"What the hell are you talking about? You got the

wrong party, bud. We ain't in that sort of business."

People were strolling past on the sidewalk unaware of the drama unfolding inside the car.

"When the hell was this supposed to have happened?" said his partner.

"Friday about 2am on Laurel."

"Friday? We left you at the Vermont on Sunset, about eight, dressed the way everyone was, we figured you'd be tied up for the evening. How the hell did you happen to be out on Laurel?"

A certain amount of doubt was beginning to creep into Frank's mind, but he wasn't about to go into details of his evening with Lois. "Never mind that. What do you mean you left me on Sunset? If you guys have got any ID, now would be a really good time to show it."

"Sure," the driver agreed. He raised his hand slowly, slipped it into his inside pocket, produced a small wallet, and flicked it open. The bold blue letters read FBI. His partner followed suit.

"That convincing enough for you?"

"I guess so," said Frank, reluctantly lowering the .38. "It doesn't answer my original question though."

The driver kept his eye on the gun.

"Threatening an FBI agent is a Federal offence, buddy. I do hope you have a permit for that piece."

"Oh, this," said Frank. "Sure I got a permit. Anyway, it's not loaded."

The two agents looked at each other incredulously.

"Okay," said the driver, his face softening. "I guess we

do owe you some sort of explanation. Sure, we've been tailing you indirectly for about a week, but we sure as hell didn't try to run you down on Friday. In fact we weren't even in town the rest of that night and the week-end. We didn't pick up on you again till just this morning."

A number of possibilities began to occur to Frank as he clipped the .38 back under his arm. "What other car do you use when you're not driving this one?"

The driver answered. "We don't have no other car buddy. The bureau ain't that generous."

"So you haven't seen a green Plymouth sedan in your travels then?"

"Sure we've seen it. He tailed you for the better part of a week, but we figured we'd scared him off."

"That is until Friday," rejoined his partner. "He must have seen us leave and figured that was his chance."

"Okay, okay," said Frank. "Now, are you guys going to tell me what the hell this all about or not?"

The two men exchanged glances.

"Well, Frank - it is Frank isn't it?" said the driver. "This is really FBI business, but I tell you what we're going to do. We're going to let you guess. If you're as smart as we figure, you should be able to put it all together."

"That very generous of you, fellas. Let's see if I can perhaps hazard a guess. Uncle Edgar sent you down here to keep an eye on his ex-agent Mr Turrou and to see that all those nasty Bund members don't stop the filming of that splendid piece of propaganda they call "Spies over America." And when you said, indirectly, a few moments ago, that meant you were really tailing this guy in the green sedan who for some reason seems to have taken a very strong dislike to me. Did I leave anything out?"

The driver glanced at his partner again with a half smile on his face.

"There you go, Frank. Our trust in you wasn't misplaced. Of course, we couldn't really make any comment."

Frank had his hand on the door lever.

"I guess I'll be getting along. Oh, did you say you had been out of town at the weekend?"

"We did."

"So you won't have seen the morning papers?"

"No. Why?"

Frank slid out of the car and leaned on the window.

"There's a newsstand back on the boulevard. I suggest you pick up a copy right away. Don't worry about me by the way. I'm going to the office, then out to Warners. Feel free to catch up any time. Bye, fellas."

Frank had gone before they could reply, but his mind was a jumble of thoughts as he got back into the car. Just when you think you are about to solve one problem it turns into two more. He had to admit these guys had taken him by surprise, although it suddenly became obvious where they fitted into the game. On the face of it the reasons for their involvement seemed pretty plausible, but in another way it posed more questions than it answered. For instance, who the hell was the mystery man in the green sedan? And why, exactly, were the FBI following him? He had a hunch this was the key to the whole case.

Frank parked the La Salle in his usual spot and walked back up toward Sunset. He wondered just how the two FBI men would react when they found out Ullrich had been murdered while they'd been off chasing some other case. It was just possible, after all this, that Jack Warner might decide to pull the plug on the movie. If that happened, Mr Hoover was not going to be at all amused.

Across the street the man in the grey Ford two-door watched as Frank entered the building.

19

There was a different guard on the gate this morning as Frank checked through. He wasn't sure how long his pass would be valid. By tomorrow he might find himself on the outside. He tried not to think about it. The first thing he noticed was the two Los Angeles County police cars in the parking lot.

As he entered Ullrich's outer office he caught a glimpse of Lois, she looked pale and shaken. Two detectives Frank had never seen before were questioning her.

"Who are you?" said one.

"Frank DeMarco, I've been working for Ullrich. Is Lieutenant Brady around?"

"Okay, I heard about you. Brady's through in there." He jerked his thumb toward the inner door. Frank gave

Lois a reassuring glance, then went in.

Brady was sitting behind Ullrich's desk in a pensive mood gazing at the sheet of paper in his hand. That did not prevent him from chewing diligently on a stick of gum. His hat lay on the corner of the desk. Harrigan was conducting a search of drawers and cupboards.

"Find anything, Phil?"

He had already guessed what Brady held was the most recent letter. Frank's eyes scanned the desk top. There was no sign of the other two notes. Lois must have managed to carry out his instruction. He wasn't usually in the habit of withholding material evidence, but if the original two notes were just hoaxes, as he now suspected, there was no point in complicating the issue. If he found out otherwise, then it wouldn't be difficult to find a way to introduce them.

Brady shifted his glance up toward Frank and moved some gum around his mouth. "Looks like everything you told us checks out, but Malone was right," he said conversationally. "These guys didn't waste much time. The date stamp on this envelope is last Tuesday. Not much of a warning there, is there, Frank?"

Frank took a seat in one of the chairs opposite the desk and put on his best nonchalant look. "Not a whole lot, I agree. But the movie was announced to the press on Friday and the story appeared the following day. They might just have been a bit miffed that Ullrich hadn't paid any attention."

Brady swivelled back and forth on the chair, relishing

his role and chewing all the while.

"Don't you think it seems a little extreme, though?"

Frank was unequivocal. "Didn't you say the department had sent some of your people undercover to check out these Bund meetings?"

"I did."

"Doesn't that go someway toward answering your question?"

Brady lapsed into silence again.

"Seems to me there's a whole lot more to this than meets the eye," he mused.

More than you know, thought Frank. After his run in with the FBI men that morning he now knew some of it. But he hadn't really had time to think it all through in context. The outline of events he'd given them still lacked a good deal of detail. He tried to kept his face non-committal.

"I'm sure you're right, Phil," he replied earnestly.

Brady chewed away for a moment.

"Seems Miss Cain might have been the last person to see Ullrich alive."

The sentence hung in the air. Frank managed to get out a cigarette and light it, to mask his surprise. "Really?" he said.

"Yes. Apparently Ullrich called her over to give her some alterations he'd made to the script. He wanted her to get in early and type them up ready for that morning's filming."

"And did she?"

"Did she what?"

"Type them up."

"Oh, yes," said Brady absently. "I got Harrigan to check. So for the moment it would appear to put her in the clear. Still makes her the last person to see him alive though."

"Barring the killer?"

"Yes, of course, barring the killer."

Frank did not have time for further thought. There was a tap on the door and the writing team of Al Field and Bert Greenberg entered.

"Lieutenant Brady. You wanted to talk to us?"

"Yes, come in," he waved a hand. "See you later, Frank," he said, which meant goodbye.

Frank took his cue and smiled grimly at the two writers as he left. There were no jokes this morning.

The news that Lois had been to see Ullrich on Sunday evening had come as bombshell. His mind raced back over the weekend's events. There hadn't been an opportunity for her to tell him since the murder and prior to that it would have had no significance.

The two detectives were sitting in reception writing up their notes. Lois was busy typing in a detached sort of way. She looked up as he came out.

"Frank, isn't this all just terrible?"

"Pretty awful, I agree. Look, Lois, have you had lunch?"

"Ah...No I..."

"Do you mind if we go to lunch?" Frank called over to the two detectives.

"Hell no, go ahead."

Frank waited until they were out of sight before he kissed her on the cheek. She still looked anxious.

"Frank, you know I was probably the last one to see Ullrich alive?"

"Yes, I heard. Brady said. He's an old colleague from the department, by the way."

Frank tried to sound casual. "Had you ever been over to his house before?"

"Only once about a month ago for a similiar thing. Something he wanted typing up ready for a morning production meeting."

Frank decided not to probe any further on that question for the moment. As they walked along the corridor Frank saw the figure of Milton Feldman coming toward them. He'd lost his slouch and he looked taller. He strode by without a word.

"Where's he going in such a hurry?"

"Maybe he wants to try Ullrich's chair for size," said Lois. "I wouldn't put it past him."

"Well, it's all rather academic. You managed to remove the other two notes then?"

"Yes, only moments before the police arrived. I've put them in the miscellaneous file. They should be safe there for the time being," said Lois. "You didn't say why you wanted me to do that?"

"It's a long story, but I think they just complicate the

issue. They can be discovered again if need be. By the way there's something I meant to ask you before. When I talked to Al and Bert they mentioned the previous writers on the picture had been fired. Do you know who they were?"

"No, I don't offhand, but I could find out from the personnel files. You think they might have written the notes?"

"Possibly. Might have been their way of getting even. They certainly had a damn good motive."

"Hmm... you could be right."

They walked for a moment in silence each thinking their own thoughts. "Any news on whether the movie will go ahead?"

Lois gave a wan smile. "It's easy to see you haven't been around the movie business long, Frank. Can you imagine the free publicity this will give the studio? Unless I miss my guess they'll have it released within a few weeks."

"That soon?"

"Well, they are in the last week of shooting."

"I didn't realise they were that close."

"I think they've been pushing ahead as fast as they could in spite of the sabotage attempts."

"Won't Ullrich's death hold things up?"

"Not when someone like Jack Warner's in charge. By the way, he's called a meeting of all the personnel associated with the movie for this afternoon. Your name's on the list."

"Me?" said Frank in surprise.

"Sure. You didn't think there was anything went on around here he didn't know about."

Frank's grey eyes moved coolly over her face.

"Not everything, I hope."

There was a hush as Jack Warner walked onto the stage of the preview theater and spoke into the microphone.

"I'm sure you all know why we are here today. Karl Ullrich was a very fine producer and I know all of you will be saddened by his death. I don't propose to go into any details regarding that, the police are working on it and I expect you to give them every cooperation.

Our best way of hitting back at the people responsible is to produce the best movie we can, and expose them for what they are. We have disregarded and will continue to disregard threats and pleas intended to dissuade us from our purpose. We have defied and will continue to defy any elements that may try to turn us from our loyal and sincere purpose of serving America.

I'm sure that Karl himself would have agreed wholeheartedly with this, and would have wanted his work, and it was his work, to be the best it could be. And I can assure you that his name will be foremost on the screen and this film will be dedicated to both him and Joe Kaufmann, who, as you know, was murdered by the Nazis in Berlin. Their names will not be forgotten by this studio.

Thank you very much."

There was a buzz of conversation as he left the stage and everyone stood up to leave. As they filed out a secretary approached Lois.

"Oh, Miss Cain, do know if Mr DeMarco is here?"

"Yes," she replied. "This is him."

Frank smiled rather vaguely.

"Mr DeMarco, Mr Warner would like to see you in his office right away, if you can?"

"Certainly."

This was the last thing Frank had expected. Maybe he'd get a chance to see this thing through after all.

20

"Who the hell are all these guys?"

"Don't you ever go to the movies, Phil?"

"Naw. Only when the wife wants to see *The Thin Man* with William Powell and Myrna Loy."

Frank chuckled.

"I'm afraid you'll have to wait for a case over at MGM before you can see them."

He and Brady were standing on the backlot of the studio where they were filming the final exterior shots of the movie. The area was an incredible sight. Within yards of one another there were Western saloons, New York streets, medieval castles, railroad stations, part of a Mississippi riverboat and a stretch of jungle. And that was just all they could see. Filming was going on in at least two of those sets.

Brady popped some fresh gum in his mouth and turned to Frank. "I heard you saw the big white chief today. Are all the rumours true?"

"What rumours?"

"They say he screws a starlet a day up there in his private office."

"Now where did you hear that, Phil?"

"Oh, you know how news travels in the department, Frank."

"I can confirm I saw him, Phil, but there was no sign of any starlets. I think perhaps he may just have a little too much on his mind today."

"How's that, Frank?"

"It would appear that he and a couple of the stars, who he didn't name, have also had similar letters. It appears our Nazi friend has been extra busy."

Brady looked incredulous.

"Is this going to be official?"

"No, it isn't, Phil, so you can forget it right away. They figure they got all the publicity they can handle. You ask anything they'll deny it. So forget I told you."

Brady's look changed to skepticism. "I take it that means they're still going to go on with the movie?"

"Absolutely. All this affair has done is make Jack Warner more determined."

"So what else did he say?" Brady asked sourly.

"Oh, he wants me to continue on the movie, try and find the saboteurs, and get a lead on who killed Ullrich."

"Well, is that all," said Brady sarcastically. "That

shouldn't be too hard, Frank. Who knows, if you succeed, they'll probably make that into a movie."

"Don't worry, Phil. If it comes down to it I'll offer you a part."

On the set they were getting ready for another shot.

"Right," called the director. "Everybody in position. This is going to be a take."

"Silence on the set," came another voice. "Okay, we're rolling."

The clapper boy stepped out front.

"Spies Over America, scene 109. Take seventeen."

"And...action!" called the director.

They watched the scene for a few moments before Brady turned to Frank. "So what's this movie all about?" he whispered.

"Last year the FBI smashed a Nazi spy ring in New York and arrested a whole bunch of them. You must have seen it in the press."

"Can't say I remember."

"You see the guy sitting next to Feldman, the assistant producer?" Frank pointed him out.

"Yeah."

"That's Leon Turrou, the ex-FBI man who was in charge of the case. He's played by Edward G Robinson in the movie."

"Did you say ex-FBI?" said Brady.

"Yeah, apparently Hoover fired him for writing a series of articles for the *New York Post*. Seems he doesn't like his operatives taking personal credit.

Anyway the articles are what the movie is based on."

"So what does the great J. Edgar Hoover think about all this?"

"Well, that's the strange part. He now appears to be encouraging the studio to make the movie. If you ask me," said Frank, "I can see the hand of FDR behind this."

"What about Warner's, why are they so keen?"

"I think we got a hint of that at today's speech. Last year the Nazis dragged the Warner film representative, Joe Kaufman, out of his office in Berlin and beat him to death."

"Well, shit, I didn't know that."

"This is Hollywood, Phil. Movietown. Dreamsville. Not many people notice what's happening in the real world."

Brady was reflective. "Puts this whole damn thing into a bit more perspective though."

"I guess it does, Phil, I guess it does."

They stood silently for a time watching the scene.

"Say," said Brady. "Who's that guy? I'm sure I recognise him."

"If you mean the tall, smooth-looking one, that's Neville Beaumont. Plays all those suave types that make women faint in the aisles. Not the sort of profile you can forget. He plays one of the spies."

"My wife ain't gonna believe this. Come on, let's go, I've seen enough."

They walked off back towards the front office.

"Come to any shattering conclusions, Phil?"

"Come on, Frank, you know better than to ask that."

They walked on in silence.

"One thing I will say though," said Brady. "This Nazi shit might just be the sort of smokescreen a killer would find irresistible."

"Possibly, Phil, possibly."

Frank knew Brady was a bit slow and methodical but he always got there in the end. Frank, however, had a head start on this one. He knew about the other notes, and the possibility of something in Ullrich's past. Not to mention the guy in the green Plymouth, whoever the hell he was. And, last but not least, those other jokers in the pack, the FBI.

Frank felt a bit of a heel holding out on Brady, but that would pass. That's how it was when you played on different teams.

Frank watched from the window of Lois's office as the two police cars departed. There comes a point in every case where possibilities became probabilities, but that didn't make it any easier to decide which was which.

Lois was standing by his side. "How long do you think all this will go on?"

"Hard to say, Lois. But things are moving pretty fast now, so I don't think it will be too long."

"What sort of things?"

"Well, I haven't had time to tell you yet, but I had a run in with the FBI this morning."

"The FBI?" she said.

"Yes, seems they've been tailing me for some reason since this whole thing began. Or at least that's how it looks."

"Following you? Why would they do that?"

"When I asked that this morning they weren't very forthcoming. But I'm working on it." Frank was playing his cards pretty close to his chest. So far he hadn't told her about the attempt on his life after he'd left her on Saturday. No need to worry her unnecessarily.

"Do you think this is all connected with the movie?" she asked.

"I'm ninety percent certain of that. But of course it is possible someone else could have gotten to Ullrich. There were the other notes, remember, but I have a feeling they could have just been a bad joke on someone's part, which is why I asked you to hold them back."

"Do you think I should get rid of them?"

"No, not yet. Let's see how things pan out. I'm going to have a chat with our two friends in the writing department. I've a feeling they know more than they've been telling. Oh, that reminds me, did you get the other two names I asked you for?"

"She reached across her desk and retrieved a sheet of paper. "Their names are Sanford and Harper. I checked them out, they weren't out of work for long, they got taken on by Paramount."

"Right, said Frank. "It'll be interesting to see what their story is."

✴ ✴ ✴

The writers building seemed unnaturally quiet, as if in some sort of reverence at Ullrich's death. Frank dismissed that thought from his mind almost immediately. These guys were a lot of things but being reverent wasn't one of them.

He raised his hand to knock, but decided that a bold entrance was required. He opened the door and walked straight in.

"Afternoon, gentlemen."

Both looked up in surprise from the typewriters they were banging away on.

"Surprise, surprise," cried Bert. "The Lone Ranger. We were wondering when you'd get around to another visit."

Frank raised his eyebrows in mock surprise. "Oh, why is that?"

"You can't fool us, we know you've been working with the cops."

"How do you figure that?"

"That Lieutenant today. He asked us if we knew anything about that threatening letter Ullrich had received."

"So?"

"Well, that's why you're really here isn't it?" went on Al. "It stands to reason you would have known all about it, along with the sabotage."

Frank smiled amiably. "You're partly right. I did know about the letter, but the cops didn't become involved until the murder. Believe me, I try to keep out of their way."

"So he didn't report it, then?"

"No. Ullrich thought it was a bluff, you know just to scare him. I have to admit I thought so too. I just can't see what anyone would hope to gain. Surely whoever it was must know this won't stop the movie."

Frank's eyes scanned each face in turn, looking for the slightest sign that they were hiding anything.

"Not a chance in hell of that." Bert was adamant. "You heard old Jack's speech this afternoon. You can bet he'd lay down all *our* lives for the movie."

"Yeah," said Al. "That's the sort of thing he's really good at."

"Of course," said Frank imperturbably, "someone else could quite easily have killed Ullrich, for a completely different reason. Something that had nothing whatsoever to do with the movie."

Bert opened his mouth to speak then closed it again. The silence was palpable.

"Is this a gag?" said Al finally.

"I don't think so," said Frank. "Just imagine it as one of your scripts. What's that one you're reading now?"

"Oh this. A murder mystery.....but.."

"Tell me, is the killer obvious or is he one you'd never suspect?"

"Well, one you'd never suspect, of course, but this is fiction...."

Frank smiled as he broke in. "I know art is supposed to imitate life. But what's wrong with life imitating art?"

"Is this leading somewhere?" asked Al.

"Yes, I suppose it is. The cops don't know this yet, but I guarantee they will within twenty four hours. Our friend Ullrich was involved in some scandal in New York before he came here, and I'm willing to bet both of you know what that was."

For a moment there was silence as Bert and Al looked at one another, as if trying to decide who was going to do the talking.

"Frank," said Bert. "I think there's something you're not telling us here. Was Ullrich being threatened by someone else?"

"Why do you ask?"

"Because that letter the Lieutenant had related only to the movie."

"How did you know that?" said Frank. "I'm sure the Lieutenant didn't show you the letter or tell you what was in it."

"No, he didn't. But it was on the desk in front of him. I'm very good at reading things upside down, I get a lot of practice sitting opposite Al here."

"Ullrich did in fact mention another letter he received some weeks ago, but he threw it away." Frank purposely used the singular, he was not about to reveal any more of his hand than he needed. "So I come back to the question I asked you. What happened in New York?"

Bert shrugged. "I guess there's no harm in telling you now in the circumstances. There was a girl in the play he was producing. She only had a small part, you know, first break and all that. Anyway it soon became obvious she wasn't up to it, but Ullrich persevered and kept her on. After a time it became impossible and he dumped her."

"Then what happened?"

"At first there were some tantrums, but Ullrich refused to change his mind. Then she disappeared and everybody forgot about her."

"And?" Frank pressed.

Bert looked distinctly unhappy. "About a couple of months later we heard she had committed suicide, took an overdose apparently. The police came around asking some questions, but nothing happened, and luckily for the show the press never made any connection."

"That's all?"

"All we know."

"What was this girl's name?"

Bert looked at Al. " Jean something, wasn't it?"

"Jean Paul," said Al softly.

Frank nodded and took out a cigarette. "Was that her real name?"

Bert opened his hands. "I assume so. Could have been a stage name, I guess. These young kids use them all the time."

Frank flicked back the top of the lighter.

"Had Ullrich been having an affair with this girl?"

"There was a rumour. But if he was, we never saw any evidence of it."

The cigarette end glowed in the flame.

"Well if he was and someone else knew about it, that might be a good enough motive for murder, might it not?"

"I guess so," agreed Bert. "That means there's the possibility of two killers after Ullrich. Who do you think killed him?"

Frank blew a cloud of smoke in the air.

"Maybe whoever got there first, Bert."

21

The overnight rain had left the city feeling clean and fresh, producing a typical early spring morning that went a long way toward reviving the spirit.

The traffic was flowing, the sidewalks were busy, rain or shine it was business as usual. Hollywood could never be accused of not knowing what its priorities were: making movies and making money.

Over at Selznick International in Culver City, filming of *Gone With the Wind* was about to resume after a seventeen day hold-up while they changed directors. Nearby, at 20th Century Fox, John Ford was directing Henry Fonda in *Drums Along the Mohawk*. At Warners Humphrey Bogart and Kay Francis were getting ready to star in *You Can't Get Away with Murder*, another hot gangster movie and so it went on.

Hollywood was so used to a diet of celluloid murder and mayhem that when it happened for real no one was quite sure how to react. So, if anyone was affected by the violent death of Karl Ullrich, there was no outward sign of it.

None of these thoughts, however, occupied the mind of Lieutenant Brady as he drove toward the Ullrich house in Beverly Hills where the jacaranda trees were just beginning to bloom.

He was thinking about a rumour he'd heard that the Feds had got a copy of the report on the Ullrich murder from the DA's office. It wasn't often that their paths crossed, but when they did there was always trouble. If Malone found out about it he'd be incandescent. The question was, what possible interest could the FBI have in a movie producer's murder? Unless, of course, all that stuff he'd seen yesterday was spilling over into real life. People didn't usually go about knocking off guys like Ullrich just because they didn't like his last movie.

Brady parked in the driveway behind several other police cars, picked up the case file and went inside. Harrigan was in the kitchen talking to a middle-aged Mexican woman who was sobbing quietly into a handkerchief. He looked up as Brady came in.

"Morning, Lieutenant," he said noticing Brady's quizical glance at the woman. "This is Mrs Hernandez, she comes in every Wednesday to do the cleaning. She hadn't heard about the murder, she never sees a newspaper, so she turned up this morning as usual."

"She any help?"

"Not really. She usually came and went when Ullrich was at the studio, hardly ever saw him."

Brady looked slightly baffled. "If she hardly ever saw him, what the hell's she crying for?"

"Probably 'cause she'll lose her job."

"Yeah, I guess. How'd she get paid?"

"Ah, the housekeeper, a Miss Carmen Diaz. I saw her Monday after you'd gone downtown with DeMarco. Came in every day about 5.30, bought all the groceries and stuff and did meals when necessary. Ullrich would always leave instructions."

"No other staff?"

"None. Unless he was having people to dinner, then outside caterers would be called in."

"Hmm...Anything else?"

"Well, it appears Ullrich had a regular lady friend who came quite often. Although, according to the housekeeper, there were others in between."

"Who was the regular one?"

"She was sure it was someone from the studio named Linda. Never knew her last name."

"That rings a bell. I'm sure there was a Linda on the list Ullrich's secretary gave me yesterday." He flicked through the file he was carrying, found a sheet of paper and ran his finger down the list.

"Yeah, here it is. Linda Salisbury, a publicist, whatever that is. We didn't see her yesterday. They said she was off sick."

Harrigan scratched his big head. "Hey, Lieutenant you know what I think. If this guy had all these other dames here maybe this Linda found out and decided to bump him off herself?"

"Alright, Harrigan, let's leave out the speculation for the moment. I'll have a talk with this Linda as soon as possible. You check out the neighbourhood?"

"Just the immediate properties, and they're pretty far apart. Access is easy, anybody could have walked around the house, there's not a whole lot in the way of security. Everybody keeps pretty much to themselves. All they appear to do is have long breakfasts by the pool, play tennis and swim. They don't, as one remarked sarcastically, spend time looking out of windows."

Brady unwrapped a fresh stick of gum, put it in his mouth and chewed thoughtfully. "So nobody saw anyone or anything unusual on Sunday night?"

Harrigan consulted his notebook. "The guy opposite arrived home around nine-thirty, said he wasn't certain but thought there was a Yellow cab waiting in the drive."

"What do you mean he wasn't certain? Either he saw it or he didn't."

"Well you can't actually see the whole drive from across there, I checked. So all he saw was part of the trunk and the rear fender."

"Did he see it leave then?"

"No, he didn't look out again all evening."

"Hmmm...I can't quite see our killer arriving in a Yellow cab, if that's what it was. Still we'd better check it out. Anything else?"

Harrigan flicked over the pages of his notebook.

"Well, probably nothing but the lady next door, who usually walks her dog every evening, saw a green sedan parked some way back up the road. Around ten she reckons. But it was gone when she returned. She only mentioned it because people don't usually park in the roadway."

"This was Sunday, right?"

"She was pretty certain."

"Any idea of the make?"

"None. Said she couldn't tell one car from another."

"Could've been somebody visiting. Check it out see if you can get any other sightings. I'm going to swing by the studio, see if I can catch up with this Linda."

"Right, Lieutenant. I guess we can let this lady go?" He indicated the still tearful Mrs Hernandez.

"Oh sure....and, Harrigan, when you get back to the office, I want you to check this guy Ullrich out, everything you can dig up. If there's anything in this guy's past I want to know about it. What, when and where, right?"

"You got it, Lieutenant."

22

Much to Ellie's relief, she was still a little nervous after last week's attack, Frank had decided to spend the day at the office. There was paperwork to catch up on, and a number of other cases had come in all demanding attention.

This was one of those moments when Frank began to feel the loss of his partner. There had been so much going on, he hadn't had a great deal of time to think about Tony in the last couple of weeks. He felt a little guilty about that, especially since the body was still lying on a slab down at the morgue. There was one consolation, however. Brady was still on the case, he and Tony had been quite close at one time, and he wasn't likely to give up.

Frank looked up. Ellie was standing in the doorway,

and she was smoking again.

"Angel?"

"Nothin. It was just I was getting so used to coming in here and looking at an empty chair, I thought maybe I'd better check to see if you were really here."

"Well, I am. But it's nice to know I engender such loyalty."

"Hey, what does that mean?"

"Alright, it's nothing rude," said Frank soothingly. Ellie's evening correspondence course obviously hadn't covered everything. "Now, did you find out anymore about Ullrich?"

"Oh, him. Yeah. There was some girl in the cast of the play he was producing. Halfway through rehearsal she was fired. A couple of weeks after that she committed suicide. No real evidence of any connection. Anyway they're sending us copies of all the newspaper reports."

"That's all?"

"Ain't that enough?"

"Sure. It just confirms what the writers at the studio told me yesterday."

"What writers?"

"You know, those guys who worked on the play with Ullrich in New York. It was only because you found out there was some scandal that I was able to get them to talk."

Ellie's face lit up. "So I did okay?"

"Sure you did. But I got a couple more things for you to do."

Ellie tossed her head. "Fire away," she said.

"According to these guys this girl went by the name of Jean Paul. They couldn't confirm it, but I'm guessing that might have been a stage name. If so, I need her real name. Then there's a guy at the studio named Milton Feldman, fancies himself as the next boy wonder. See what you can find out on him."

Ellie face had changed to a frown. "Hey, that don't sound so easy, boss, but I'll give it a shot. Might take a lot of long-distance calls though."

"That's okay, Ellie. We are on expenses."

About one-thirty Frank decided to go out for sandwich and coffee. It was also about time he checked out the two names he'd gotten from Lois. She'd said the two guys fired by Ullrich were working at Paramount, which, if he remembered correctly, was over on Melrose, only a few blocks away.

Sanford and Harper turned out to be another couple of comedians who gave a slightly different version of the events leading up to their dismissal. According to them they told Ullrich they were leaving because they'd had a better offer. Ullrich got mad and told them they were fired and to leave immediately, which meant they were out of work for a couple of weeks before they could start here at Paramount. Frank was inclined to believe them since they had a pretty solid alibi. Being down in San Diego working on a picture when Ullrich was killed seemed about as solid as you could get. Still that didn't mean they were out of the frame. They could still have sent the notes, they freely admitted they still had contacts inside Warners.

Whether it was a good thing or a bad thing he wasn't quite sure, but this case had more suspects than a gangster B-movie.

On his return he set about writing up a full report on the case so far. Jack Warner was going to want to see something for his money. Frank was certain Jack knew all about the earlier threats to Ullrich, although they seemed slightly less relevant now, so there was no point in keeping anything from him. After all he was the client now. Ellie, for her part, had been spending long periods on the phone. The afternoon wore on.

Frank was smoking a cigarette and contemplating his argyle socks and Florsheim brogues which were perched on his desk, when Ellie stuck her head round the door.

"It's nearly five, Boss, and I got a date for the movies tonight. Okay, if I go?"

"Sure," said Frank, raising a hand. "Dare I ask what are you going to see?"

"*White Heat* with James Cagney."

"Not another gangster movie, Ellie. You'll soon be talking out of the side of your mouth."

Ellie made a face and left.

It was well after six when Frank finished off the report and slipped it into the tray for Ellie to type up next day. He poured himself a shot of Old Plantation from the bottle in the drawer and walked over to the window. A slight cooling breeze came in from under the raised sash occasionally stirring the vanes of the dusty venetian blind. For a long time he stared down at the moving pattern of cars on the boulevard. Writing everything down had crystallized his thoughts, but this case had taken so many twists and turns it was hard to see where it would all end. He had a hunch, though, the end wasn't all that far away. But, as with everything, you needed that little bit of luck.

By the time he turned away it had begun to get dark. He finished the drink, rinsed out the glass in the sink in the corner and put the bottle away. The building was quiet as he left, the night operator was already on duty and took him down to the lobby. At the far end of the hall a cleaner was at work. Most other businesses kept normal hours.

Outside as he lit a cigarette his thoughts turned to Lois. She'd been invited out to dinner this evening by some big star from the studio. Frank didn't like it, but there wasn't a whole lot he could do about it. He didn't own any part of her, nor she of him.

He had just turned down Ivar when it happened. His preoccupation with his thoughts meant he heard the footstep and the movement behind him a little too late, he felt something hard and blunt dig into his spine.

"Hold it, pal," a gruff voice demanded.

Frank stiffened. A wave of sour breath came over his shoulder.

"Put your hands on top of the car," said the voice again.

Frank swore softly to himself. "Okay," he said. "What is it you want?"

"What we want is for you to keep quiet," said the voice. A hand frisked him expertly and found his shoulder holster.

"He clean?" said another reedy voice.

"He is now," said the first one removing the snub-nosed .38 from under Frank's arm and dropping it in his pocket.

"Okay, move fella, move."

He prodded Frank roughly toward a big, black four-door Packard sedan parked a little way down the street. He tried to get a glimpse of the license plate, but it was in deep shadow. Not that it would have done him much good to know in the circumstances, but old habits die hard.

The second man opened the rear door as the first hustled him along the seat and followed him in. The door slammed shut with a sort of grim finality. A passer-by glanced curiously at the car, then quickly looked away, not wanting to be involved.

"Now, you just sit tight, Mr DeMarco and everything will be fine and dandy," the man in the fedora rasped.

Frank didn't blink an eye at the mention of his name. The other man, who had a slight but noticable stoop, got quickly in behind the wheel and slammed the car into gear. With a lurch and a screech of tires they pulled out from the curb and sped off down the street. At the junction with DeLongpre they made a fast left and headed east. They crossed Vine and El Centro in quick succession before turning left again at Gower. Heading north now they crossed Sunset, then Hollywood skipping a light on the way. They were moving fast, the driver working at the wheel and muttering occasionally as slower traffic got in the way. Frank could see the needle flickering high on the dial.

Frank's attention, however, was soon focussed on something a lot more dangerous than his captor's bad driving. Pointing at him in the back seat was a .357 Magnum Python, which, according to Colt, was the fastest, most powerful and best-looking handgun you can own. Frank wasn't about to argue with the quality of their advertising. If fedora man pulled the trigger on that cannon, he'd take out anyone in the line of fire for at least a block.

Frank sat back and studied him in the dim light through lowered lids. He was heavily built and wore his dark-brown fedora pulled well down. His fleshy mouth was raised at the corners in a slight sneer, his eyes dark and watchful.

Traffic was thinning out as they hit Franklin and made a quick right.

Frank summoned up his most confident voice, not easy in the circumstances, all the while keeping his eyes on the man and the gun. "Would somebody mind telling me where we're headed?"

The driver looked up. Frank caught a glimpse of him in the rearview mirror for the first time. The face was long and sharp with a bluish jaw, the eyes were as cold and empty as a tiger shark. "You'll find out soon enough, fella," he sneered.

They made another fast left onto Los Feliz and in a few moments turned sharply left again. Frank knew for certain now they were headed into Griffith Park, and that wasn't good. "Aren't you guys interested in what I might know?"

Fedora man regarded him balefully. "Look, bud, what you know or think you know ain't no concern of ours, so just keep quiet."

An icy finger touched his spine. There was no mistaking their intent. Another thought chilled him even more. These might easily be the guys who killed Ullrich, or even worse, Tony. Then something else flashed across his mind, a man leaving the building the day Ellie got sapped. It had to be the same man. Frank's eyes aquired the hardness of blued steel.

They were up in the hills now and as the big car coasted along the last street light vanished. The bright glow from the city was all that illuminated the interior. For the last few minutes the driver had been glancing in his rearview mirror.

"Everything okay?" asked fedora man anxiously, noticing.

"Yeah, sure. Some lights been with us since the start,

but they've gone now. I think we lost them on the boulevard."

This could be the chance Frank had been waiting for, just a tiny lapse in their concentration, but he needed something else to divert attention.

"Mind if I smoke?"

Fedora man fixed him with a stare. "Go ahead, buddy, if it'll calm your nerves, but be very careful."

Frank pulled out a crumpled green-colored pack of Luckies, put one in his mouth and patted his pockets for a light. As he did so he felt the pressure of the slim, bone-handled throwing knife against his side. He waited. The driver glanced in the mirror again, and for a moment fedora man took his eyes off Frank. In a second the razor-sharp blade was in his hand, he swung it in low gleaming arc with as much power as he could muster, his left hand clamping down on Fedora's gun arm like a vice.

"This one's for Ellie."

The man, eyes open wide in surprise, looked down at the knife which had suddenly appeared below his shoulder and gave a dry gurgle.

"You son-of-a-bitch," he gasped. His instant reaction was to pull the trigger as Frank's hand wrestled the gun around.

There was a big, flat crack and a vicious spurt of flame from the ventilated barrel as the .357 Magnum slug angled off through the front seat. If the driver had bad posture, he wasn't going to have to worry about it much longer. With a muzzle velocity of 1430 feet per second the slug from the Colt Python destroyed two of his vertebra, sliced through his liver and intestines, blew a fist sized hole in his abdomen and carved its way halfway through the engine block.

The car slewed crazily across the road as the driver lost control, the wheel spinning out of his limp hands. They hit a low bank at the roadside, bounced over and careered off down the slope.

Fedora man slumped down in the back seat his eyes closed the gun dropping from his nerveless fingers.

"Thanks for the ride, boys, but I think this is where I get off." Frank didn't wait a second longer. He grabbed for the rear door handle, forced it open and threw himself out onto the grassy scrub curling up as he went. The car careered on down the incline for another ten yards before smashing into a clump of trees.

Frank knelt on one knee to regain his breath, then stood up slowly. He checked himself over. His shoulder hurt and he had a few bruises, but nothing was broken. He took a deep breath. The chill night air had a sharp fresh scent. Above him the stars glittered like they had on every other night since creation. They had ceased glittering, however, for his two erstwhile friends for the evening.

There was no movement as Frank approached the wreck. The only sound was the hissing of steam from the radiator. Fedora man's body lay half out of the back door, hat gone and shirt soaked in blood. From the way his head lay Frank knew his neck must be broken. The driver, wedged under the dash, must have been dead before the Packard hit the tree, but if he wasn't the steering wheel had crushed his chest.

Frank glanced quickly up toward the road as some headlights swept by. But no one appeared to have noticed.

He quickly retrieved his gun and knife, wiped his prints from the door handle with his handkerchief and went through the pockets of the man in the rear. There was a cheap billfold with a few dollars, a driver's license showing behind a celluloid window, nothing else apart from loose change, some numbers slips and a cheap keyfob. He held up the license and could just make out a name in the dim light. Alfred Neumann. He was about to return it when he noticed a folded piece of paper tucked in behind. He slipped it out and returned everything quickly to the dead man's pocket.

Oblivious, the stars glittered on brightly as he scrambled back up the slope. In the distance the floodlit shape of the Griffith Observatory stood out against the hills.

23

Hollywood nights.

From the upper floor dining room of Cyrano's on Sunset Strip the view across the city was a fantastic sparkling carpet of light that looked like it went on forever. Few people could fail to be impressed by it. Over on Hollywood Boulevard searchlight beams restlessly probed the night sky above Graumann's Chinese theater.

Lois sat taking in the scene from one of the tables surrounding the pale wood dance floor, trying not to show how impressed she really was. Everything around her just sparkled with style. The decor was sleek streamline Moderne, a gleaming black staircase led up from the bar and booths below. The upper parts of the walls were painted with exotic jungle scenes reminiscent of Rousseau. Across the room on a raised black dais Benny Goodman and his band were playing one of the latest swing numbers. This time is was the real thing, not a studio crew.

In truth she was far more impressed by the man sitting opposite her. More than once she had to pinch herself to believe this was actually happening. Not in her wildest dreams when she'd set out on her mission to Hollywood had she imagined where it might lead. Sitting opposite her, dressed in a black tuxedo and white tie, was Neville Beaumont, movie star, someone she'd only ever seen previously on the screen.

It had taken a good deal of hard work, patience and not a little charm, before she'd landed the job with Ullrich. Especially without any previous experience of the movie business. But it was surprising how quickly one learned the ropes, provided you saw yourself strictly in the role of an observer and not a participant. Keeping a sense of reality, however, when surrounded by all these movie stars was not an easy task, even for her.

She'd sensed Beaumont's eye on her from the moment she'd bumped into him on the set. His reputation with women was second only to that of Errol Flynn. Although not a leading man, his smooth and charismatic style knocked them dead in the aisles. After several approaches she'd finally given in to his charm. Lois was perfectly well aware she was about to enter the lion's den. It was a price she was prepared to pay.

A bottle of Bollinger sat in a cooler by the table and

from time to time the waiter topped up their glasses. She glanced up from the menu in her lap and brought the glass to her lips. Beaumont was tall, dark and sophisticated with the perfect Hollywood profile. A touch of grey at the temples only added to the distinguished effect.

"Now, Lois, have you decided what to order?"

A waiter hovered in the background awaiting a signal.

"I think I'd like the cream of cucumber soup and the shrimp creole.

Beaumont raised a finger. The waiter was instantly at his side notebook poised.

A few moments later, with the ordering out of the way, Beaumont looked appraisingly across at Lois. Such poise and confidence. He still could not believe that someone as beautiful as this wasn't a star.

"Well, what do you think?"

"Beats anything we have in Indiana by a mile," replied Lois taking in his gaze.

"So would I be right in thinking you haven't been here before?"

Lois smiled. "You're right, I haven't."

Beaumont was even more amazed.

"Forgive me," he laughed. "It's just that most new arrivals in Hollywood are brought here in their first week. A sort of initiation."

"I see. Well, I'm just an ordinary working girl, with no such aspirations."

Beaumont leaned across the table. "You, my dear, are

anything but ordinary. I'm sure half the people here at the moment are wondering exactly who you might be."

"Good heavens. Why would they do that?"

"Don't you realise that most of them are the big shots of the industry, producers, directors, or agents whose main aim in life is to beat their rivals to the next big star. They probably make as many deals here as they do in their offices."

"Do they really?"

"You can bet on it," he smiled. "Ever done any acting yourself?"

"A little Shakespeare at college. Nothing earth-shaking."

"So am I to assume you didn't come to Hollywood to get into movies?" he sounded surprised.

"Not really. Oh, don't get me wrong. I love the movies, the whole business is so terribly exciting. It's just that I feel the magic wouldn't be quite the same if I were in part of it myself. I know you'll think that sounds very silly, but there it is."

Beaumont looked at her, his eyes curious. This was a new experience, a girl who didn't actually want to get into the movies.

"No, certainly not," he agreed. "Quite the reverse. There are other things in life." He stood, held out his hand, and pulled Lois to her feet. "Let's dance," he said.

On the floor Lois spotted a number of well known faces, but there were still quite a few she didn't know. They were the real heavyweights, the producers, directors and agents who could make you or break you. Beaumont whispered a few of their names, Myron Selznick, John Houston, Eddie Mannix. Mostly they didn't mean anything to Lois, nor would they, this wasn't going to be something she intended doing for the rest of her life.

Another couple danced by.

"Isn't that Jack Warner?" whispered Lois. "Do you think he'll recognise me?"

Beaumont smiled. "Possibly, but he's more likely to offer you a contract."

Lois smiled a little nervously. At this point in time the most important thing was to keep her job. There was still some unfinished business to attend to. They danced, dined, and danced again. The evening sped by - she felt like Cinderella at the ball.

It was after 1am when they left. Outside the club a group of diehard autograph hunters clamored for their attention. There were a few screams when they recognised Beaumont. When they were seated in the sleek black Cadillac and pulling away from the curb Beaumont spoke.

"You will come back for a nightcap?"

"If you insist."

He leaned over and kissed her lightly on the cheek. "I most certainly do," he said.

The interior of Beaumont's house in Beverly Hills turned out to be richly furnished with lots of dark wood, white walls, and wrought iron, light years away from the cool Moderne style at Cyrano's. The living room had a sloped ceiling with exposed beams and a massive stone fireplace. A log fire blazed merrily away. Someone had obviously anticipated their arrival. A huge picture window looked out across a flagstone terrace toward the emerald glow from the swimming pool.

The first thing Lois had noticed was the painting in the hallway.

Beaumont paused. "Do you like it?"

"The Cezanne? Yes, beautiful, isn't it?"

Beaumont's eyes widened. Not many of the women who'd seen the picture on their first visit even noticed it, far less knew who the artist might be. As he guided Lois into the living room for that nightcap he had only one thought in mind, this was one conquest he really was going to enjoy.

Lois awoke suddenly and instinctively glanced at the clock. It was 2.35am and the space beside her in the bed was empty. She sat up and glanced around the room. In the half darkness she could make out the shapes of furniture. At the far end of the room a faint line of light came from under a doorway. Beaumont must have gone to the bathroom. She slid back down into the warmth of the bed. Just a minute, she thought, the bathroom door was on the right - the light was coming from the left, the dressing room. What would he be doing in there?

Her curiosity was aroused.

She slipped out of bed, not stopping to put anything on, and crossed the deep pile rug which covered most of the floor. The dressing room door in heavy oak plank with wrought iron handles, matching those of the bathroom opposite, was slightly ajar. Her hand reached out and pushed it gently open. It moved silently, on well oiled hinges.

The central light had not been switched on, the glow appeared to be coming from the far end of the room. She moved in a little further, peering around the edge of the wardrobe. Light was coming from behind the full length mirror on the back wall which angled away concealing an opening.

Her mouth opened and her throat became dry. It looked like some sort of hidden room. There was a faint murmur of a voice within.

She stood frozen in the sheer drama of the moment. Then she began to shiver violently, not helped by the fact that she was completely naked. She pulled the door gently to and fled back to bed. It was a good five minutes before she stopped shaking.

A little later she felt the bed move as Beaumont returned, slipping in quietly so as not to disturb her. Her eyes tightly closed, she kept as still as possible and feigned sleep. It was quite some time before she drifted off.

24

Someone had noticed.

Frank could see the lights of a sedan parked up about twenty yards back on the shoulder. As he came up the slope the doors opened. Two figures emerged. They were dark shapes against the city lights.

Then a voice called. "DeMarco, is that you?"

With a wave of relief Frank recognised the voice of one of the FBI men. He sure as hell didn't need any strangers at a time like this.

"Yeah," he called back, hopping across onto the roadway. It was then he noticed the glint of light from the gun in the man's hand.

"We're sure glad it's you, because if it'd been one of those other sons of bitches we'd have blown his goddamn brains out right here and right now," said the

FBI man hitching back his jacket and holstering his gun.

Frank gave a grim smile. "I don't think you have to worry about either of them," he said. "They've gone into permanent retirement."

"You want we should go down and check?"

Frank brushed himself down and shook his head. "No need. Say, how'd you guys happen along?"

"Get in the car, Frank, and we'll tell you. We don't want to get caught out here if anyone comes along. You alright by the way? You look a little messed up."

He held the car door open.

"I'm fine, just a few cuts and bruises. I'll survive." Frank said dryly, as he slid into the rear seat. "We can't keep on meeting like this, though. We haven't been formally introduced."

The driver quickly got back behind the wheel, leaned over the bench seat and held out his hand. "I'm Merv Curtis and that," he said, flicking out a finger at his partner, "is Lou Fisk."

Frank returned their handshake. "Thanks for the timely rescue, fellas, but you didn't answer my question."

"Well, Frank," replied Curtis. "We've been checking on you from time to time as you know from our last meeting. We just happened by this evening when we saw those two bozos pick you up. We thought we'd better tag along just in case."

"Why didn't you butt in then?"

"No time, Frank," joined in Fisk briskly. "Besides we couldn't risk a shoot out in the street. It might have got you killed and our car full of bullet holes. Mr Hoover is very picky about things like that. So the best we could do was follow, see where they were headed."

"Yeah," came back Curtis. "We nearly lost you when they turned off Los Feliz. That guy was traveling pretty fast and he must have spotted me. But I had a hunch they'd head into the park. We were way back though, when we saw the tail lights go over. You had us worried there for a moment, Frank."

"Never mind you, I had me worried there for a lot more than just a moment. Those guys had me down for a one way trip."

"Hey, Merv," butted in Fisk. "Shouldn't we get outta here? You know I called this in. Those prowl car boys will be along any minute."

Curtis looked quickly at Frank. "This might be a stupid question, but did you leave any evidence down there?"

"Materially, no. But they might just wonder how the guy in the back seat managed to stab himself in the shoulder."

"Well, we'll let them wonder, shall we?" said Curtis, swinging the car around in a tight turn and heading back down the hill. As they turned out onto Los Feliz they heard the sound of a siren. A few moments later a prowl car with twin spotlights went tearing past.

"There go the cavalry," said Fisk.

"Right on cue," said Curtis.

Frank knew there was little love lost between the Feds and the local cops. He was suddenly aware, however, that they had him in a very tight spot if they ever chose to make use of their information.

Frank's car was still parked on Alta Vista where he'd left it. Curtis pulled in behind and stopped. He switched off the lights and put an arm over the back of the seat.

"Before you rush off, Frank, to do whatever it is you gotta do, we need to ask a few questions. Okay?"

Frank nodded. "Those I can answer, I will."

"Can you tell us exactly what happened?"

"This gonna go into some official report?"

"Only as information indirectly obtained."

"Right. Since I figured these two charming fellows weren't taking me out there for an early birthday surprise, I played the only card I had."

Frank gave a brief description of events, ending up with the retrieval of the gun and knife and including the fact that he'd wiped his prints off everything he knew he'd touched.

Curtis's face slowly split in a wide grin. "Straight out of the manual, Frank, I got to hand it to you. By the way that's a mighty handy blade you carry there."

Frank gave the coolest smile he could muster. "You know what they say, it always pays to have an edge."

"In more ways than one, I'd say," said Curtis.

Frank's smile expanded a little. He still wasn't quite

sure how this was going to play out.

"You make either of these guys?" asked Fisk.

"Yeah, as a matter of fact I did. The one in the back went by the name of Alfred Neumann, least that's what his driving licence said. I recognised him, I'm pretty sure he was the one who broke into my office last week and sapped my secretary. As for the driver, no idea. He was out of sight beneath the dash."

Fisk looked concerned. "Sapped your secretary, what the hell was that all about?"

"Maybe they thought there'd be some paperwork on them, or something, nothing else I can figure." Frank decided not to mention the slip of paper he'd removed from Neumann's wallet. He wanted to check that out himself. Besides, it could turn out to be nothing at all.

"Well, you seem to have managed fine on your own," said Curtis again. "And there we were worried about you."

Frank was beginning to appreciate these two, but he was still well aware he was on the outside looking in.

"Do I get to ask some questions now?"

"Fire away. Those we can answer we will." smiled Fisk.

"You said you caught a glimpse of them when they picked me up. Had you seen them before?"

"Definitely not," answered Curtis. "They appear to be new players in the game, but if you think about it, you might guess what rock pool they crawled out of."

"You mean they were Bundists?"

"What do you think?" replied Fisk.

"Why exactly, do you imagine, were they trying to kill me?"

Curtis and Fisk exchanged glances, Frank knew right away he wasn't going to get a straight answer. Curtis's face became serious.

"Look, Frank, the most we can say is they think you know something, when in fact you don't. Which, I suppose, could explain why they searched your office."

"This something you're talking about. Do you know what it is?"

"Most of it Frank, most of it. But we can't really say any more at the moment," said Fisk. "I hope you can understand."

"Well, I suppose half an answer is better than none. Mind if I go and get cleaned up now?"

"Certainly not, Frank. Go ahead. I hope you're on expenses though, those pants don't look too good."

"Thanks again, fellas," grinned Frank. "I'm sure we'll be running in to one another again quite soon."

"Bet on it, Frank. Bet on it."

The first thing Frank did when he got back to the apartment was take a shower. He needed time to relax and think. The next thing was to pour himself a stiff Scotch on the rocks and think some more. A game could go on for a long time with no strikes, then they all came in the last quarter. Tonight he had had a lucky escape. If it hadn't been for the FBI, he'd be Malone's guest in a cell downtown.

Those two bozos in the Packard had obviously not got the idea of taking him on a one-way trip by themselves. The first attempt on Laurel had been opportunistic, the last had been carefully planned. The question was, were they connected to Tony's murder or Ullrich's? Or, maybe both?

He sat down on the bed, switched on the radio and looked again at the small slip of paper he'd removed from Neumann's wallet. It had a printed number on one side and written in pencil on the other was G.R. 507 Metropole. The seven had a little line through it, that funny way they do in Europe. The paper itself appeared to be of no significance. It was pale yellow in color with one serrated edge and looked like a hat check receipt. Just something handy to note a hotel room number on, for that's what he assumed it was. And, unless he was very much mistaken, the letters were someone's initials. The Metropole, if he recalled correctly was down somewhere on Spring, not exactly the best part of town. But it was a lead, he thought as he rolled into bed. However slim.

Frank lay back and listened for a while as the radio talked about the dangers of the coming war in Europe, then switched it off when it began to extoll the virtues of Bromo-Seltzer.

25

The following day dawned dull and overcast. Earlier, Beaumont who had been picked up by the studio limo, had taken a short detour and dropped Lois off at her apartment. It had given her time to shower and change before going to the office.

Now, wrapped in her white towelled robe, she headed for the small kitchen, brewed a pot coffee and brooded about the fact that Beaumont might be some sort of foreign spy. In all her imaginings she could never have dreamt of anything so bizarre. It sounded like something out of a dime novel. It occurred to her that it could be just some sort of game, but she had to admit that seemed highly improbable.

The shower had helped her relax, but hadn't done a lot to solve her dilemma, and her gloom was unrelieved by the grey skies which left her normally sunny kitchen dull in the early morning light. Her mind vividly replayed the events of the night before, some of which she was already beginning to regret.

After her discovery in the dressing room the night had passed in fitful slumber. Fortunately Beaumont had not made any further demands upon her. That morning he had risen quietly about 6am, dressed and gone downstairs, presumably for an early breakfast.

Left alone in the bedroom she had dressed quickly, then, unable to resist her curiosity, had sneaked back into the dressing room for another look. In the half light everything looked normal, the mirror panel on the wall was closed. Had she not seen it for herself the night before, she would never have noticed anything untoward. But it had yielded after a few pushes and the panel had clicked open revealing in the dim light a spacious little cubbyhole, a desk a chair and what was obviously a powerful radio transmitter.

She had stood for a moment in shock, then closed the panel and returned quickly to the bedroom, her mind in a turmoil. In the bathroom she had checked her face and hair in the mirror, composed herself, and made her way, as calmly as she could downstairs. Beaumont had been pacing rather impatiently in the hall. Her performance had been worthy of Joan Crawford.

She recalled the chain of events that had brought her here in the first place and the lives that had been changed forever. Now, as she sipped her coffee and stared out at the profusion of pink flowering oleanders outside her window, her mind returned to the problem at hand. It was way outside the brief she'd been given but she knew there was really only one thing to do. She rinsed the cup in the sink, checked the number they'd given her in the small diary she carried in her bag and went through to the telephone.

"Hello?" she said.

"Field office," a laconic voice answered.

"I'd like to speak to Mr Simpkins, please."

"Who shall I say is calling?"

"Lois Cain."

"A moment please."

Lois fidgeted with the belt of her robe. Then a tired sounding voice came over the line.

"Yes, Miss Cain, this is Simpkins. Before you say anything, can I first ask where you are calling from?"

"From home."

There was a small click on the line.

"Very well," replied Simpkins. "What can I do for you?"

"I have to talk to someone as soon as possible. Something has come to my attention. It's very important."

There was a short silence.

"Very well, Miss Cain. I'll have to arrange something. Will you be at the studio later?"

"Yes," said Lois, quickly glancing at her watch. "As usual after nine."

"Fine. I'm going off duty now so Curtis or Fisk will call later this morning. They will give the usual password. All you have to do is confirm the time, the meeting will be at the usual place. Okay?"

"Yes. Thank you Mr Simpkins."

She put the phone down and found she was trembling.

It was Curtis who called.

"Hello?"

"Miss Cain, I believe you're free for lunch."

"I am," she replied. "12.30?"

"Fine."

The receiver clicked off.

After the cloudy and dull start the day was, at last, beginning to brighten. Lois took a Yellow cab from the rank outside the studio. It took only around ten minutes to get to the Scenic Gardens which lay just off Franklin Avenue, by which time the sky had returned to its traditional blue. After all this was California.

She paid off the taxi, entered the park and walked to the bench where Curtis was already seated, engrossed in the crossword of the *Los Angeles Times*. His partner Fisk was loitering nearby.

Curtis looked up from the paper as she approached. He had dealt with a lot of contact people in his career, but none as drop-dead gorgeous as this. She wore a white linen tailormade with dark blue edging. The hemline was the latest style, finishing just above the knee.

He tried to concentrate as she sat down next to him and crossed her long nylon clad legs. He was sure his pulse rate had just doubled.

"Miss Cain," he acknowledged.

"Mr Curtis." She paused, her mouth relaxing in a quick smile, "I have no intention of going into any detail of how I came by this knowledge, so you will have to take what I'm about to tell you on trust."

Curtis looked into those cool blue eyes and wished he was Gary Cooper. "Go ahead," was all he said.

She told him purely and simply about what she had seen in the Beaumont house, leaving out all the events leading up to it.

Curtis sat for a long moment before he said anything. Then he placed the folded newspaper on the bench beside him and pulled a black spiral bound notebook from his inside pocket.

"You have the address of this house?"

"Yes," she said without hesitation. "1364 Brookwood Drive, Beverly Hills."

"Can you describe exactly which room the main bedroom is, from the top of the stairs?"

"Yes."

He outlined it on his notepad as she described it. Then showed her.

"That look right?"

"The proportions are larger, but that's it."

"Anything else?"

She gave him a brief resume of the police visit to the studio and what little she knew of Frank's investigation.

"That's all, I think," she concluded.

Curtis looked into her eyes. "If what you say is true and I have no reason to doubt it, then this could be extremely valuable information. We will of course have to check it out, but be assured no one will know we've been there. I'm sure I don't have to remind you not to repeat anything you just told me to any other person."

"I am aware of that, Mr Curtis."

He stood up and put the paper under his arm. Fisk, who'd been lounging under a nearby tree, came and joined them.

Curtis looked at Lois again.

"We'll drop you off back near the studio."

Lois gave him a pale smile.

26

The forensic report on Ullrich had arrived at 10.15am. It was on Brady's desk when he came back from the interview room. They had a suspect in custody over a number of hotel room burglaries. Something else to add to his case load. He picked it up. It took him the next ten minutes to read it through.

"Harrigan," he yelled. "Get in here a minute."

"Hold on, Lieutenant. I'm just taking a call."

Brady flicked through the rest of the Ullrich file as he waited. He was studying a photograph of Ullrich's desk when Harrigan came in.

"That was the M.E. on the phone. He wants us to go and look at a couple of stiffs they got down there."

Brady put Ullrich's photograph down in irritation.

"What the hell for?"

"Seems they were brought in after a traffic accident in Griffith Park late last night. Routine, so they thought. Turns out the driver didn't die in the accident, he was shot in the back."

"By who?"

"You're not going to believe this, he was apparently shot by the guy in the rear seat who himself died of a broken neck. But here's another twist, he had a knife wound in his shoulder."

"Who had?"

"The guy in the rear seat."

"Who the hell stabbed him?"

"Well, they surmise there must have been a third person in the car, but there's no trace of him. They're checking the car now for prints, but there's no other evidence at the scene."

"They ID either of these bozos?"

Harrigan looked at his notebook. "An Alfred Neumann and a Max Hart."

"Shit," said Brady. "I suppose we'll have to go and take a look. If anything else happens around here, we might as well start moving our beds in." The forensic report lay on the desk in front of him. "You read this yet?"

"Not so far, Lieutenant," said Harrigan. "Print boys find anything?"

"Only what you would expect. DeMarco's prints on the patio door and the telephone. The rest are accounted for; the staff and Ullrich himself."

Brady stared at the photograph he had just picked up

before he went on. "There's something odd though."

"What's that?"

"Look there," he said pointing. "Five silver frames on the desk top, but the one you can see in the background has no picture in it."

Harrigan looked and nodded his head. "Okay, but so what? Maybe he just got tired of looking at it."

"Possibly, possibly, but that's not what I meant. According to forensic," he turned up the page, "all other frames were smudged with prints, but this one had none."

"None at all?" said Harrigan.

"None at all. So whoever removed the picture didn't want his prints showing and wiped it clean. Hardly something Ullrich would do himself. Besides, if he'd removed the picture, he'd be unlikely to leave the empty frame on his desk."

Harrigan wasn't the world's greatest brain, but quite often he hit the nail on the head. "You think the killer could have removed the picture because it was someone he didn't want us to see?"

A thin smile touched Brady's lips. "You've got to admit that's a distinct possibility...maybe a picture of him and Ullrich together?"

Harrigan screwed up his face. "Could be, but it doesn't really tie in with the Nazi angle though does it?"

"No, that's true. Maybe the picture has got nothing to do with it at all. There's probably some innocent explanation for it, but it's a loose end and I don't like loose ends." Brady leaned back in his chair and unwrapped a stick of gum. "Another thing bothers me. I can't see these Nazi guys using a .32. It's too much like a woman's weapon."

Harrigan was enthusiastic. "Now that is a possibility, Lieutenant. It could point to something a lot more personal, like this dame Linda, for instance. Maybe it was her picture in the frame. What did she have to say by the way?"

"Well she seemed pretty upset. Said she knew he had other women, the temptation was too great when you're a producer. She didn't like it, but she accepted it. Says she stayed Friday and Saturday, but left Sunday after a late breakfast. Doesn't fit the timeframe of course, but she could easily have gone back. No real alibi either, said she did some work, had an early dinner then went to bed. But you never know. What else we got?"

Harrigan was glancing through his notes. "I assume the report confirms the time of death between ten and twelve?"

"It does."

"Okay. The secretary says she left about nine-fortyfive. That would tie in with the sighting of the Yellow cab, if we accept that is what the witness saw. The green sedan, which no one else noticed incidentally, was seen around ten."

Brady chewed ruminatively. "That makes everything pretty tight. It also makes the secretary the last person to see him alive barring the killer, so, unless he was

Superman and dropped into the back garden outta the sky, this guy in the green sedan is all we got."

"Looks that way, Lieutenant."

"That check you're running on Ullrich. Did that throw up anything?"

"Nothing so far. According to Warners he came out here from New York just over a year ago after producing some play on Broadway. I checked NYPD, they got nothing on him. You want me to dig some more?"

"Hmm...You could try a call to immigration. See what they have on him. It might tell us something."

Harrigan scribbled a note on his pad.

Brady waited until he finished. "Now what about the Senna case? Anything new on that?"

Harrigan leafed through his pad again. "Not really, apart from finding out the property belonged to Warners, one of several they own and let out to stars or cast. This one is unlet at the moment, so whoever was using it was doing so illegally."

Brady stroked his chin reflectively. "Funny, don't you think, Warners name cropping up in both these cases."

"You think there could be a connection?"

"Naw, don't see how there could be."

"Just a coincidence then?"

"Yeah, just a coincidence," said Brady shrugging. There was a note in his voice that showed he wasn't all that convinced.

※ ※ ※

Just about the same time as Brady and Harrigan were reviewing their evidence, Frank was driving across town to the Metropole. As the lone tower of City Hall came into view he could see some dark piled-up thunderheads moving in off the Pacific. When they hit the mountains there'd be some more rain.

Before he left he'd checked with the hotel to see who the house dick was. It turned out to be an ex-cop named Nick Crowley, who got fired for drinking on the job. Frank had worked with him back when he was on the force.

He'd been doing a lot of thinking since last night's attempt on his life. The FBI man's clue about what the killers thought he knew was intriguing. He could only imagine it was something connected with Ullrich's murder. But what? Since this was strictly an FBI play, there was no way of knowing at the moment. Curtis and Fisk hadn't actually said the two men in the car were Bundists, but there was now little doubt in Frank's mind. However, he had to admit this was only supposition. So far he hadn't got a shred of proof for any of it.

Curtis had also said that they were on the verge of some discovery. Frank had no way of knowing what that was. The big question was, had the Feds just been playing nursemaid to Leon Turrou or were they after bigger fish?

The Hotel Metropole, an eight story brownstone building on the corner of Seventh and Spring, had an air of faded elegance about it. It had long since been deserted by the rich and famous for places like the Roosevelt and the Beverly Hills.

Frank angled the La Salle into a spot opposite the hotel and parked. The early morning rain had gone, but there were still a few puddles on the sidewalk.

Crossing the entrance lobby, with its old brown leather chairs and potted palms, he went up some shallow steps to where a blonde stood behind the reception desk. He was about to ask for Nick Crowley, when a voice behind him said "Never thought I'd see you down here, Frank."

"Nick, how the hell are you?"

Crowley was a big broad shouldered man with short ginger hair, thinning now on top. His face had a ready open smile. "Come on through," he said. "The bar ain't open yet, but we can get a drink."

Frank hesitated, obviously not much had changed. "Sure. A bit early, but what the hell." They walked toward the darkened bar. "You been in this place long?"

"Yeah, too fucking long. One of these fine days I'll chuck it in."

After they were seated in the dimness of the lounge with a couple of bourbons in front of them, Nick spoke again.

"I was sorry to hear about Tony by the way. A damn shame. It was a shock to read it in the papers. You find the bastard yet?"

"Well, you know that's cop business Nick. Brady's on

it. A tough one to crack though."

"I know Brady, he's a good cop, not like some I could mention." Crowley took a mouthful of rye. "What brings you down to my neck of the woods then, Frank?"

"It's a long story, Nick, and I won't bore you with it. I came across a Metropole room number in a case I'm working on. I wanted to check it out."

"What was the number?"

"Five-o-seven."

"You got a name to go with that?"

"No, but the initials may be G.R."

Crowley knocked back the rest of his drink. "I'll go take a look."

He was back in three minutes.

"According to the register 507 was occupied by someone called George Ritter."

"Well, the initials are right. Did you say was?"

"Yeah. Checked out this morning."

"Checked out? What time?"

"About an hour ago."

"Do you know long he'd been registered?"

"About three weeks, I'd say, give or take."

"You ever see this guy?"

"Not that I can remember, Frank. We got a lot of guests here. Although quite a few are regulars, the place is partly residential and the rest are transients. Anything else I can do for you?"

Frank finished off his drink and stood up.

"Any chance of seeing his room?"

"Frank you know that's against the rules," replied Crowley with a slow smile. "But what the hell, you're buying the drinks. Come on, I'll get the key."

"Any use asking why you're interested in this guy, Frank?" he said as they entered the dark panelled elevator car.

"Just a long shot. He could be just a bookie or running a floating crap game. Who knows?"

"You can be damn sure of one thing, Frank."

"What's that?"

"He wasn't running no crap games in my hotel."

"I believe you, Nick, I believe you."

The elevator jerked to a halt on five and the doors opened. They turned and walked down the narrow corridor. Room 507 was the last door on the left. Crowley stuck the key in the lock and opened it up.

"Looks like you got lucky, Frank, maid service ain't been through yet."

Frank grunted. That was pretty obvious, the room was in mess with the bedclothes in a rumpled heap. It looked like friend Ritter had departed in some haste.

Frank checked around methodically. The drawers in the bureau were all empty, as were the nightstands. The wastebasket in the corner, however, contained a screwed up copy of today's *Los Angeles Times*.

On the front page was a big black headline and a photograph of the accident in Griffith Park.

27

Frank and Crowley exited the elevator and strolled toward the front desk. "Any chance the clerk would remember what this Ritter looked like?" asked Frank.

"I guess," said Crowley. "He only checked out just over an hour ago."

It was the same girl who'd been on the desk earlier. She looked up in interest. Blonde, well built, in her late thirties but trying to look younger, with pale golden hair cut in a bang across her forehead. Her full lips gleamed red. She eyed both men in turn, her gaze lingering just a fraction longer on Frank.

"Hi, Nick," she said, her gaze switching back.

"Stella, this is a friend of mine, Frank. A private eye. He's interested in the guy in 507 who checked out earlier this morning.

"Oh yeah, how's that?"

"Just a case I'm working on," said Frank. "Can you give me some idea what this guy looked like?"

Stella frowned a little. "About your height and build," she said. "Wore a dark blue suit and a grey fedora. That's about it."

"What about his face and hair?"

"Sandy sort of hair, what you could see of it. Cold blue eyes though, looked right through you." She smiled sweetly. "Not like yours."

Frank returned the smile. He knew this was all he was going to get. "Thanks a lot honey. You been a great help."

She looked after him wistfully as both men went down the steps and moved through the main lobby to the front entrance.

"Still able to charm the broads I see, Frank."

"Some of the time, Nick, some of the time."

They paused at the top of the short flight of steps to the sidewalk. "If this is the guy I think he is, he must have had a car. Where would he have kept it?" asked Frank.

"Well, the hotel park is pretty small. We usually send clients over to the all night garage on Hill Street. You could try there. Tell them I sent you, it might help."

"Thanks, Nick. I owe you one."

"Any time, Frank. Take care."

A few minutes later Frank was walking down the ramp at the parking garage, a couple of blocks over from the Metropole. The guy in the glassed-in booth wore a dark blue blazer with gold buttons. He looked bored. There was a matchstick in his mouth.

Frank stood by the window.

"Yeah?" said the man removing the match, and trying to look interested. "What car you got?"

"No car. I just came from the Metropole. A guy registered under the name of Ritter checked out just over an hour ago. Nick Crowley, the hotel dick, thinks he might have kept a car here."

"Who's asking?" he said, carefully inspecting the end of the match.

Frank slid a five out of his clip and put it on the window shelf.

"Abe Lincoln's asking."

The man's eyes flicked down toward the five dollar bill. The corners of his mouth moved up in faint grin. "Well, let's see. If he was the last guy to leave, like you said, I think it was a grey Ford two-door."

Frank frowned, that wasn't the answer he was expecting. He didn't release his finger on the bill. "Is this the same car he's been using for the last few weeks?"

The man furrowed his brow and thought some more. He didn't take his eye off the five.

"Naw, now you mention it. Just these last few days. Before that it was a green Plymouth."

Brady and Harrigan were waiting in the office when he got back.

"Well, Frank," said Brady. "We'd just about given up on you."

Frank stuck his hat on the stand, went round behind his desk and sat down.

"You should have made an appointment, Phil. Anyhow I never knew you to give up on anything."

Brady crossed his legs, placed his brown fedora carefully on his knee, and took out a pack of Luckies. "Care for a cigarette, Frank?" He pushed the pack across the desk. "Got a light?"

Frank put a cigarette in his mouth then patted both his pockets. "Hmm... seem to have lost my lighter someplace."

Brady produced a stainless steel Zippo, flicked back the cap and held out the flame. "This wouldn't be it, would it?"

Frank took the light. "Could be Phil. They all look pretty much alike. Where did you find it?"

Brady held it between his fingers, flicked the top back and forth a few times, and placed it deliberately on the desk. "Harrigan found this one in Griffith Park."

"Griffith Park?"

"Yeah, I figure it must have fallen out of your pocket when you jumped outta that black Packard last night."

Frank kept his face straight, but compressed his lips in a thin smile. Brady had certainly surprised him, but it couldn't be anything more than an inspired guess. If there'd been any identifiable prints on it, he would have said.

"I guess you must mean the accident in Griffith Park. All I know about that is what I read in the *Examiner*." Frank knew he was on thin ice here. If the FBI chose to reveal what they knew he was in big trouble. "As for the lighter," he went on, "could be anybody's

"Possibly Frank, possibly. Something else, though. You still keep that trick knife up your sleeve like you used to?"

"Now and again as the occasion demands."

"Well let me tell you what I think. The occasion did demand. Those two guys were taking you for a ride, possibly, without a return ticket."

"You seem pretty sure about that, Phil."

"Is Roosevelt a Democrat?"

Frank kept the amused look on his face. "Go on," he said.

"We checked out those two dead hatchet men and guess what we found?"

"I'm still listening, Phil."

"They were fully paid up members of the local Bund, in other words playing in the same ballpark as you and Ullrich."

"How do you figure that?"

"Harrigan here recognised them from one of the meetings he went to undercover. They were both sitting up front acting like security for the big boys."

Frank glanced across at Harrigan, who seemed more interested in the Vargas calendar on the wall.

"This is all very interesting, Phil. Tell me, why exactly

do you think those two hoods would be trying to kill me?"

"Well, apart from some possible connection with Ullrich, that's why Harrigan and I have been sitting here all this time hoping you would tell us."

There had been no doubt in Frank's mind as to their identity, but at least Brady had confirmed it.

"Sorry, I'll have to disappoint you there, Phil." He was thinking furiously. Brady had made up quite a bit of ground, he wasn't exactly breathing down Frank's neck, but he was getting close. "Talking about Ullrich, you got anything more on the murder?"

"It's just possible those two might be our boys, but we can't very well question them now, can we? Anyway they must have used a different car, so we're checking that out."

"What do you mean, a different car?"

"Well, we had a report of a green sedan parked down the street from Ullrich's place the night of the shooting. This morning we had a report of a damaged green Plymouth dumped over in Long Beach. The rental company reported it stolen, the guy gave a false ID, but we haven't checked it out yet. "

"A green Plymouth?" repeated Frank, a little too eagerly.

Brady looked instantly suspicious. "You wouldn't happen to know anything about that now, would you, Frank?"

Frank sat quite still for a moment. Pieces of the

puzzle were beginning to fall into place.

Brady spoke again. "If you do know anything about it, you'd better say so now. I won't be able to keep this from Malone, and you know him, he'll have your balls along with your badge."

"If this car has a damaged nearside fender then it may be the car we're both looking for."

Brady looked incredulous. "How the hell would you know that?"

"If I'm right, for some reason this car has been tailing me on and off for the last fortnight. Late last Friday he tried a hit and run over on Laurel, which is where he damaged the fender."

"Let me guess, Frank. You didn't think it worth reporting."

"Yeah, well he missed."

"That's not all is it?"

"No, Phil. This morning after a tip-off I traced the guy and the car to the Metropole on Spring. He left an hour before I got there. Goes by the name of George Ritter. But I wouldn't get too excited about that, you won't find him in the phone book."

"Where exactly did this tip-off come from?"

"Ever heard of good detective work Phil."

Harrigan, who had remained impassive throughout, was busily making notes.

Brady stubbed out his cigarette and took his hat off his knee. "It's a cinch if this Ritter left the Metropole this morning he must have been driving something?"

Frank grinned. "A grey Ford two-door, I didn't get the plate. Looks like he's pulled a switch just in time."

Brady got to his feet, put on his hat, then picked the Zippo off the desk. "Like they say in the movies, Frank. Don't leave town."

"Thanks a lot, Phil," said Frank acidly.

Brady studied the lighter and flicked the cap back a couple of times. "One thing does puzzle me though. How'd you manage to get away after the accident?" He held his hand up before Frank could protest. "I know you said you weren't there, but someone sure as hell was. The prowl car was on the scene in seven minutes, and it's a damn long walk down through the park."

28

Harold Simpkins was and looked like a man in his forties. He had a long stony face, deep-set brown eyes and a hint of a tan. He habitually wore a double-breasted dark blue suit, a Harvard tie and well-polished wing-tipped Oxfords. Nothing ever seemed to change his melancholy expression.

Curtis wondered vaguely how his wife remained married to a man who left the house wearing the same suit every day. Mind you, perhaps that was a trifle unfair. He did occasionally wear a different tie and his wardrobe probably contained half-a-dozen identical suits, used in strict rotation of course.

Simpkins had taken over operational control after the dimissal of Leon Turrou some months back. Hoover was well aware that the discovery of the New York spy ring was only the tip of the iceberg. Unless something was done very quickly things would rapidly get out of control.

The fact that the Nazis were targeting America came as no surprise to him. They knew that sooner or later the US would be drawn into any conflict. Until then their main aim was to keep America out for as long as possible, to give them time to deal with the British. Los Angeles was a prime target with so many aircraft and defence related industries in the area, not to mention the huge propaganda value of the movies. Joseph Goebbels knew all about them. His use of Leni Riefenstahl's 'Triumph of the Will' showed that.

The FBI were operating out of a suite on the third floor of the Beverly Regent Hotel on Wilshire, which made it easy for people to come and go without undue attention.

Simpkins was seated at his desk studying several 10 x 8 blow-up prints with a glass. They showed a table covered with code books and assorted papers, among them several photostats of technical drawings. A swastika on the code book could clearly be seen. After a while Simpkins looked up.

"These would appear to be pretty conclusive. I suppose it would be pointless asking how you got these?"

Curtis knew Simpkins was a hard man to fool. "Well, sir, let's just say they just happened to come into our possession."

"Hmm...well as you are no doubt aware this constitutes an illegal search and would be useless in any court."

Curtis nodded. "We are aware of that, sir, but if we catch Beaumont with the rest of the group, then all we need is a court order to search the house and ...er... rediscover the evidence."

Simpkins steepled his fingers and looked back at Curtis. His mournful expression did not change. "It may not be as simple as that."

"I don't know that I follow...."

"This man is a top Hollywood star, Curtis," said Simpkins in a quiet but relentless tone. "His exposure may do more harm than good. You may not know it, but this man was actually born in England, although I believe his mother may have been German. Just think of what our friend Mr Hearst would do with that."

Curtis leaned back in his chair and breathed out slowly. Nothing to do with the department ever seemed to be bloody straightforward.

"What do you suggest, sir?"

"I suggest, Curtis, that other means be found," replied Simpkins somewhat icily.

Curtis knew it was useless to argue. Politics was bloody politics, and besides he was absolutely right. No one had ever said this job was going to be easy.

"Very well, sir, but we'll need a little time to figure this out."

"Time, Curtis, is not a commodity we have very much

of at present."

Curtis grimaced. "I am aware of that sir."

Simpkins shuffled through the papers on his table before finding what he wanted. "Moving on," he said "I've read the rest of your report. How much does this Cain girl know?"

"Well, no more than we've told her sir."

"And what precisely would that be?"

Curtis gritted his teeth. Simpkins could be a real bastard when he wanted. "Simply that some people, for various political reasons, didn't want the movie made and would go to any lengths to stop it. Anything she saw or heard she was to report to us. This affair with Beaumont certainly was completely out of left field. We have, as you know, long suspected some prominent people in the movie world had sympathies with the Nazis, but so far there's been no clue as to who they might be."

Simpkins nodded. "You realise that whatever solution you come up with regarding Beaumont will have to include this Cain girl as well?"

Curtis was a bit quicker out of the blocks this time. "One thought does occur, sir."

"What is that, Curtis?"

"All the girl saw in that room was the radio transmitter. Correct? No documents."

"Correct."

"What if we tell her that Beaumont was an agent working for say...the British and therefore not contrary to American interests. How would that do?"

Curtis thought he saw a trace of smile cross Simpkin's lips, but he could have been mistaken.

"Yes," he said slowly. "That could be the answer. I wouldn't imagine the Cain girl questioning that."

"There is another problem, however, sir."

Simpkins arched an eyebrow.

Curtis continued. "We'll have to talk to Jack Warner about this at some point. How much can we tell him?"

"Well, as you are no doubt aware, Warner is in the Director's confidence regarding this film and the reasons for it being made. No doubt he'll have to know the truth about Beaumont at some point. Perhaps over a period of time Beaumont could be eased out at the studio, given lesser roles, maybe. We certainly don't want any hasty action. As I already said, that might attract press attention."

Simpkins obviously didn't know Jack Warner. Hoover would have to come up with the promise of something a lot more tangible than that. They'd probably have to induct him into the bureau as an honorary agent. Badge and all.

"No, sir. I see," replied Curtis quickly supressing the thought. "Just enough truth to be plausible."

"Precisely. Now let's move on. Have we any leads on the Ullrich killing?"

"Well, we know the Nazis have been after Ullrich for some time. According to the police report a green sedan was seen about the time of the killing, not far from the house. That much we've been able to gather from our source in the DA's office. Now it's too much of a coincidence to believe it wasn't the car we've been tailing these last few weeks."

Simpkins pulled at his long face. "And where exactly is this vehicle now?"

"That's the point, sir, we've not been able to pick him up since the killing." Then before Simpkins could interject he went on, "If you recall sir, you re-assigned us that weekend."

"Hmmph. I do not need reminding, Curtis. I have no doubt whatever that whole episode was staged to draw us off while they killed Ullrich, but we had no way of knowing that at the time."

"No, sir. Quite, sir." Curtis didn't mention it, but he and Fisk had already figured that out.

Simpkins leafed through the rest of the report. "You mention this attempt to kill this DeMarco fellow by the two Bundists. Could either of them have killed Ullrich?"

"Possibly, sir, but I don't think so. Neither of them is our Nazi killer. He's probably dumped the green sedan by now, but he's still out there somewhere."

"Hmm...useful chap that DeMarco," said Simpkins absently. "So what's your next move, Curtis?"

"Well apart from DeMarco, who as you say seems well able to take care of himself, Beaumont is our only lead." Fisk appeared at his elbow and slipped him a large yellow envelope. "However sir, there may just be one other possibility."

Simpkins raised his bushy eyebrows. "Oh, what's that?"

Curtis slipped a photoprint out of the envelope, knowing it would confirm his guess. "We just had this blow-up of a photograph our man took last night. You can see it shows a list of addresses of all Warner properties in Hollywood."

He passed it across the desk to Simpkins who picked up his glass and examined it. "One has a ring around it and something penciled in the margin, looks like a date and time."

"Yes, sir." said Curtis.

"But that's for tonight."

"So it is, sir. So it is."

29

Frank pulled the La Salle into the parking lot of Harry's Cocktail Bar on Sunset around five-thirty and pondered Curtis's rather cryptic call. Somewhere we can meet to discuss something in private, he had said. He didn't want to come to the office, just in case it was under observation.

Harry's was the sort of place that had a regular clientele, although they weren't as grand as that made them sound. In fact most people who even drove by, couldn't do so without a curl of the lip. Mind you some of those people would swear, years later, when places like this became part of Hollywood's architectural heritage, that they'd loved it all along.

Frank had taken a rather circuitous route just to make sure he wasn't being tailed. After the other night's events and friend Ritter still on the loose, there was no point in taking chances. He wasn't sure what the two FBI men had on their minds, but on the phone he'd mentioned he knew something they might be interested in.

The place was fairly quiet, just a couple of guys in loud suits at the end of the bar, and midway down, a brassy-looking blonde in a tight sweater smoking a cigarette and trying to look nonchalant. She was holding on grimly to what looked like a Manhattan. Probably the only thing that was keeping her upright. The booths were little better, just a couple with their heads together talking quietly and and old guy drinking on his own.

The bartender moved himself down the bar, and wiped some non-existent spots off the counter. "Frank," he said. "We ain't seen you in a while. What'll it be?"

"Make it rye, straight up. I'm expecting a couple of friends, so I'll take it in the end booth."

"Okay, Frank. I'll bring it over."

As Frank walked over and sat down, the blonde eyed him over the rim of her glass. He made sure he sat where there was no possibility of eye contact.

The bartender was just putting the drink on the table when Curtis and Fisk walked in, trying their hardest not to look conspicuous.

"We'll just have the same," Curtis said looking at the bartender. Joe nodded, glanced at them curiously and walked away.

"Well, hello again, Frank. So this is where you hang out?"

"Occasionally."

"I expect you're wondering what this is all about?"

"So soon, I'm curious. Must be something fairly big. You look like a couple of cats who just got a large dish of cream."

The bartender put two more drinks on the table and looked at Frank. "You want to run a tab?"

"Yeah, thanks, Joe."

Curtis waited until he left before speaking again. "You said you had something to tell us. Perhaps we'd better start there."

Frank looked over his drink. "I held out on you a little the other night. There was a note in Neumann's wallet giving a room number at the Metropole, although I didn't know that until I checked it out later."

Curtis smiled and raised his glass. "I'm glad you decided to level with us, Frank. Go on."

"This guy, using the name George Ritter, checked out of the Metropole about an hour before I got there. But I did find out he'd been driving a green sedan."

"Well, now you know who tried to clip you that night on Laurel," said Curtis.

"And since we know he's dumped that car," said Fisk. "Any chance you found out what he's using now?"

"According to the guy in the garage, a grey Ford two-door."

"Right," said Curtis, "that brings us bang up to date.

His name isn't Ritter though, that's just an alias. His real name is Gunther Radel, one of those Gestapo guys you might have read about."

"Gestapo?"

"Yeah. German secret police, a pretty nasty bunch from what I hear."

"What the hell's he doing over here?"

"It's a long story, Frank, so I'm just going to give you an edited version. It will also answer your question of the other evening, because obviously you'll find out sooner or later. If our boss knew we were telling you half of this he'd have our balls in a vice. So I want your word as an ex-cop and all that, you'll keep your lip buttoned?"

"You got it," said Frank unhesitatingly. He wondered vaguely how they knew he was an ex-cop, but at the very least it meant that they'd keep the lid on the events in Griffith Park.

"According to our information, Ullrich was some sort of film-maker in Germany. Then he got in some trouble with the Nazis and made a run for it. They've been after him ever since. Anyway, a couple of years ago he showed up in New York, bummed around for a while, then got a job producing some play on Broadway. Very successful I believe. The rest, as they say is history, with that under his belt he came out to Hollywood."

Frank drank some rye. "So that's why he was so keen to make this movie."

"Precisely. But when the Nazis found out, they sent

someone out here to stop it and take care of him."

"You mean this guy Radel?"

"Right again."

Frank lit a cigarette. "How did they find out Ullrich was here?"

"We've suspected for some time there's been a spy ring operating around L.A. although we didn't have any leads. We can only assume they spotted Ullrich and sent word back to the Fatherland. So when this Radel turned up in New York, looking suspicious, immigration tipped us off and he was followed here. We've been tailing him hoping he'd lead us to them."

Frank was trying to get his head round all of this. "So why has everything suddenly changed?"

"We think we know most of the people involved."

"Are you going to tell me who they are?"

"If you agree to what we propose, you'll find out soon enough for yourself."

"That's pretty cryptic."

"Not really, Frank. Last night one of our people was able to photograph some documents. Among those documents was a list of locations with one highlighted for tonight."

"And where was that?"

"1714 Alta Brea Crescent."

Frank looked puzzled. "That somewhere I should know?"

"No reason you should, but we wondered if you might. It's one of a number of properties around

Hollywood owned by Warner Brothers."

"Warner Brothers?"

"That's right, Frank."

Frank looked levelly across at Curtis. "You may not be aware of this, but three weeks ago my partner was killed outside one of their properties on Claymont Drive."

Curtis stared across the table for long moment before he spoke. "We know that, Frank."

"You know?" Frank said hollowly.

"That was the location of the first meeting of our Nazi friends. We were tailing Radel. We saw the whole thing go down. He's the one, Frank. He killed Tony Senna."

Frank stared at Curtis, not quite believing what he had heard. "Why the hell would he do that?"

Curtis shrugged. "That we could only guess. Maybe they thought he was spying on them. We had to figure your partner was a player in the game, or why else would he be there?"

"I can tell you why he was there. He was supposed to be staking out a house on Braemont Drive, but someone misheard and sent him to Claymont Drive."

"My God, that's unbelievable."

Frank shrugged. "It happened. Why didn't you guys come forward before?"

"Our hands were tied. This whole operation could have gone straight down the toilet. The main guys took off before we could identify anyone and we had to stay put or be discovered. Everything happened so fast there's nothing we could have done to save him. But believe me, Frank, we're in this game until we get this bastard."

Frank gripped his glass. "That explains why this Radel was tailing me. When they found out Tony had a partner, they had to figure I'd be in on it."

"Precisely," said Curtis. "And they only had to check the phone book to find you."

"Where's this bastard Radel now?"

"We lost him after Ullrich's murder. You almost got him this morning, but it's just as well you didn't, it might have spoiled the party. You see, we're pretty certain the address we mentioned is where he and his friends will be tonight."

Frank finished the rye. "Why exactly are you telling me now, before you've caught him?"

"Isn't that obvious, Frank?" said Curtis, looking hard at him. "We need your help."

"Me? Frank was stunned. "I didn't think you guys issued invitations."

"Normally we don't," said Fisk. "But we got to improvise here. We only found out about this a couple of hours ago and it's got to be done quietly. Very quietly. There's a big star involved and we don't want any flat-footed cops on the scene. So to tell you the truth we're just a bit short-handed."

"Apart from that," added Curtis. "This is directly connected with Warners and we're going to need your help and a little discretion there. Also, since this bastard took out your partner, we figured you'd have the right sort of motivation. What do you say, Frank?"

Frank stubbed his cigarette out in the ashtray. "What the hell," he said. "This whole case is going down like a movie anyway."

"I take it that's a yes?" said Curtis.

"It does."

30

The sky was crisp and clear in the coolness of the early spring evening. Ahead the solid black mass of the San Gabriel mountains stood outlined against the backdrop of stars.

Alta Brea was a dead-end street off the lower end of Canyon Drive in the smart suburb of Hollywood Hills. Here and there the occasional light gleamed in the darkness from properties dotting the hillside beyond.

Seventeen-fourteen stood alone at the far end on two lightly wooded acres, cut off by a low random stone wall bordering the turning circle. The house was English Tudor style with half-timbers set in stucco around a random stone tower with deep-set, diamond pane windows. At the end of a long flagstone path a short flight of steps led up to the solid planked oak front door, with a small inset leaded window. Above was a timbered portico, in deep shadow under the overhang. The only light was a faint glow from one of the side windows.

To the right lay an empty swimming pool, leaves and debris littering the bottom. In the starlight the dark mass of trees and shrubbery surrounding the house merged into the hard black shadows on the ground. It had obviously been unoccupied for a while, but this must have been one of those Warner places reserved for big stars. It was much to smart for rank and file cast.

Out front the driveway already had two cars in it, they were indistinct in the gloom.

"Can you make out what they are?" Frank whispered, as Curtis peered through the binoculars.

"The nearest one looks like the Ford two-door but I can't make out the color in the dark."

"It's a fair bet that's the car Radel drove off in this morning," said Frank softly.

"I'm sure it is," muttered Curtis. "Now we're only waiting for the star of our show to arrive."

They had parked on an adjacent street and worked their way through the grounds of a couple of neighbouring properties to arrive unseen at the rear of the house. At first it had looked completely unoccupied, then Frank had noticed a chink of light at the edge of the kitchen window, and a faint glow from the room at the rear overlooking the covered patio. On closer inspection they discovered it to be the dining room with the table pulled out and chairs around. It was obviously set up for a meeting.

Before moving to their present position out front they had worked out their intended plan of attack. Now they just had to wait for the last car to arrive.

Frank had no illusion about the kind of people they were dealing with. He read the papers like anyone else. But this case had concentrated his mind on events that were happening on the other side of the world. He'd no idea how these events would eventually unwind, but this was his chance to make some small contribution. Apart, of course, from the personal score he had to settle. He checked again the comforting shape of the .38 Smith and Wesson Special Curtis had lent him. They didn't want any bullets ending up in anybody unless they came from an FBI weapon.

Curtis prodded Frank and handed him the binoculars, indicating he take over the watch. He focused down the empty street, dappled here and there with hard shadows from a row of tall palms, ruffling every now and then in the light breeze. Down on Canyon Drive a brief flash of headlights indicated a passing car, but so far none turned into Alta Brea. For a time they stood just waiting and listening, the tension slowly mounting.

"What time is it now?" asked Frank eventually, eyes returning to the binoculars.

Fisk glanced at the luminous dial of his watch. "Eleven minutes past eight." he whispered.

"Trust this bastard to be late," muttered Curtis.

Suddenly, as if on cue, light flared at the end of the silent street and materialized into the twin beams of an approaching car. As it drew closer they heard the soft even note of a V-8 and saw the sleek black shape of a Cadillac coupe as it slid quietly along the block toward them. It pulled onto the driveway behind the two other cars and halted, lights snapping off.

No light came on as the car door opened. Two men got out fast, hurried along the path and up the steps toward the entrance, vanishing momentarily into the shadows. The front door opened as if someone had anticipated their approach and they stepped quickly into the vertical strip of light. In a second they were inside and the door was swiftly closed.

Unknown to Frank this was a scene replaying itself. But he instantly recognised the famous profile, a glimpse of which had cost Tony Senna his life.

He was stunned. "My God," he whispered. "That's Neville Beaumont."

Ten minutes later, inside the house five men were seated at the long dark oak dining table. Tightly pulled brocade drapes covered the French doors to the terrace, contrasting with the rough cream plaster walls. In the corner stood a wrought-iron floor lamp, the only source of light.

Colonel Stauffen, security officer at the German Legation in Los Angeles, looked around the table and addressed them in his clipped English.

"I shall attempt to keep this as brief as possible. You are all perfectly well aware of the dangers involved in our meetings. Now, gentlemen, can I have your reports?"

The man on his left began. "Our man in Hughes Aircraft has reported plans for a medium-range bomber known as the D-2. It involves a new material called Duramould. No details as yet."

"Very well. Make it a priority. Next."

Just as the next man began his report on the break-in at the Martin Aircraft plant the previous weekend, there was a small sound from the direction of the kitchen.

The man's voice trailed away.

Radel half rose from his chair his cold blue eyes alert. A Walther P-38 appeared in his hand. Just then Curtis came through the kitchen doorway holding a Thompson submachine gun.

" FBI," he yelled. "Don't anybody move."

The five people sitting around the long dining table covered in papers and plans were immobile for a second. Radel's face twisted into a mask of fury, the Walther jerked up, his finger already squeezing the trigger.

At that moment the French doors were slammed open and Lou and Frank came through sweeping the heavy drapes aside. It was enough to put Radel off. His bullet splintered the woodwork a foot from Curtis's head. It wasn't the Thompson that replied, however, it was Fisk's .38. His bullet passed straight through the flesh and bone of Radel's upper left shoulder and dug itself into the wall behind. The force of the shot sent Radel staggering back against the bureau. One flailing arm caught the floor lamp which crashed to the floor, plunging the room into sudden darkness.

In the split seconds that followed the dining table went over as everyone dived to the floor. Frank suddenly realised he and Fisk were easy targets outlined against the starlight. Sheer instinct made him move.

"Hit the floor," he yelled at Lou.

Two muzzle flashes of orange fire came in quick succession from the far corner of the room. The slugs whined past Frank's head and smashed through the window pane. He cursed as he collided with an overturned chair on the floor. There were more curses and shouts all around in the darkness. To his left someone was moaning softly. He swung his arm around, encountered a body and jammed his gun into it.

"Don't move an inch," he ordered. He strained his eyes to see, but with only the faint light of the window behind him he could make out nothing in the room. There was a sudden shout in German and someone to his right scrambled up and made a run for the open French window. The Walther flamed again from the corner and with a cry the figure pitched over headlong onto the patio and lay still.

"Merv, Lou, you okay?" called Frank anxiously.

"Yeah," came their voices in unison. "Watch out

though," went on Merv, "the bastard's still got four left in that clip. I'm going to try and put the overhead light on, so get ready."

As he spoke Merv's hand was inching slowly up the wall to the light switch by the kitchen door.

"Ready now," he shouted as the room burst into light. The scene was one of total confusion with up-turned chairs scattered around and everyone lying flat on the floor. In the corner Radel, cursing in German, was struggling to his feet. He immediately began to fire wildly. Frank and Lou, who had both risen to a crouching position, replied simultaneously. Both bullets hit home, slamming Radel back against the wall.

Radel looked down for a moment in surprise and shock at the bloody crimson mess of his chest. His legs folded and he slid to the floor, leaving a long red smear on the cream plasterwork. A second reflex shot gouged a hole in the ceiling before the Walther dropped from his nerveless fingers. He didn't move again.

For a moment all eyes fixed on the body on the floor, then Frank's gun shifted to cover the room. Blue gunsmoke and the smell of cordite was sharp in the air. "Now everyone on their feet very, very, slowly."

"Where the hell's Beaumont?" shouted Lou. "He must have crawled out the doorway in the confusion."

The front door slammed.

"He's trying to make a run for it. Frank, you know what to do," ordered Curtis sharply, motioning with the sub-machine gun. Frank leapt across the room and sprinted off down the hall.

Beaumont had his hand on the starter when Frank wrenched open the Cadillac door and stuck the barrel of the Smith and Wesson unceremoniously in his left ear. "I wouldn't do that if I were you, sonny," he said softly.

Beaumont froze, his face white with fear. "Wh....what are you going to do?" he stuttered.

"Just shut up, move over and do as I tell you."

Frank prodded him roughly across into the passenger seat of the big Cadillac, got behind the wheel, and clipped the .38 away under his arm. "And don't try anything heroic," he warned. "This ain't no fucking movie."

The starter whirred.

"Where are you taking me?" said Beaumont shakily.

"What's your address?" said Frank, ignoring the question.

"I don't understand...."

"Your address," said Frank again.

"1364 Brookwood. Beverly Hills."

Frank moved quickly off down the street, swung the big black car out onto Canyon Drive and headed south. He drove fast until they hit Franklin then turned west. He'd stay on Franklin until he could pick up Hollywood Boulevard well past the centre of town. The last thing he wanted was anyone recognising his charge.

After a while Beaumont regained enough of his courage to speak again. "Would you be kind enough to tell me what is going on?" he demanded imperiously.

Frank looked across at the famous profile, one that wasn't about to be seen much in the future. "I should have thought that was obvious," he said. "They want you out of the way until they decide what to do with you."

Beaumont slumped in the corner and said nothing further until they reached the house. Frank parked in the driveway.

"What now?" asked Beaumont.

"We stay here until the morning, when you phone the studio and tell them you're indisposed."

"Do I have a choice?"

"None whatever."

"Very well," said Beaumont resignedly. "What do you suggest I tell the servants?"

"Just say there have been some threats on the picture and I'm a private eye here to guard you. That isn't all that far from the truth. I'm working for Jack Warner anyway."

A look of recognition came to Beaumont's face. "I thought I'd seen you somewhere before."

"Let's not get too pally, Neville. Jack will be pleased to hear we got that Gestapo killer tonight, but when he hears about you, he'll probably cut your balls off and nail them to the studio gate."

Beaumont's face resumed its defeated look. There were no servants around when they entered the house and halted at the bottom of the stairs. Frank produced the .38, shook out the empty shells, reloaded and spun the cylinder.

"Just remember I'll be down here, and should you think of trying anything clever, I'm sure you'll remember the mess this made of your Nazi friend."

Frank's eyes were hard as he slipped the gun back under his arm. Beaumont tried to suppress the shudder that went through him.

"Where will you sleep?" he asked.

"Don't concern yourself about me, sonny boy, I'll find a comfortable chair." He watched as Beaumont, head bowed, slowly mounted the stairs and disappeared. Frank turned on his heel, glanced at the Cezanne, before throwing open double doors to the living-room. He certainly wasn't going to worry about what Beaumont might do, with a profile that famous he'd nowhere to run.

He glanced around the room. One thing at least he ought to be able to find here, was a good Scotch.

31

It was mid afternoon when the meeting finally got under way. The temperature in Malone's office was only just short of boiling point. Present, besides him, were the two FBI men plus Brady and Harrigan along with Carmady, the assistant DA. Some extra chairs had been brought in to seat everyone.

When Frank walked into the room Malone just about burst a blood vessel. "What the hell is he doing here?"

"If you mean, Mr DeMarco," replied Curtis archly. "He is central to this case."

Malone scowled and subsided silently into his chair. "Alright, let's get this thing underway. Now, this is just an informal meeting with no record being taken. At the end we can decide what paperwork is required."

He glanced at the handwritten set of notes Brady had prepared for him. "According to this, last night one man were arrested, one man was killed, another's in hospital and the fourth was released because of diplomatic immunity."

He looked stonily across at Curtis. "I talked to some guy called Simpkins this morning. He assured me you'd be able to explain why this operation was carried out without prior notification to LAPD."

All eyes turned to Curtis.

"From the time we found out about the meeting we had at best a couple of hours to organise something. It would have been physically impossible to co-ordinate any actions between ourselves and the police in that time."

"We could still have been informed," said Malone in an icy tone.

"That's true," admitted Curtis. "However, at that point, we only had the meeting place and at best a guess that it would take place that night. Not by any means certain knowledge."

Malone did not look happy, but he accepted it. "The man you killed," he said. "Who was he?"

"He went under several names but his real one was Gunther Radel."

"Is that supposed to mean something to us?"

"No reason why it should, Captain, but he's about to improve your murder clear-up rate."

"Murder......Who the hell did he kill?"

"The first person he killed was Frank DeMarco's partner, who by some mischance turned up at the site of one of their secret meetings."

Both Brady and Harrigan jumped up.

"How the hell do you know that?" cried Brady.

"We happened to be tailing Radel at the time. We saw the whole thing go down." said Curtis calmly.

"Did you know about this?" said Brady turning to Frank.

"They told me last night, Phil."

Brady sat down somewhat mollified.

Curtis waited a moment before resuming. "They were using empty Warner Brothers properties for their secret meetings. The two men you have in custody are both employed as security men at the studio. They, of course, had access to the property list and knew which were unoccupied."

Brady threw up his hands. "So when Tony wrongly staked the place out, they assumed he was watching them and killed him."

"Right, Lieutenant, right. And when they found he had a partner," he nodded toward Frank, "they tailed him for a while to check him out. When he became coincidentally involved with Ullrich, they tried to kill him too."

"When exactly was this?" growled Malone.

"Late last Friday after a reception at the Vermont."

Malone glared at Frank. "And needless to say he didn't report it."

"That would have been pointless," cut in Curtis. "At that stage he had no idea who the driver was or why he should want him dead. Coulda just been somebody with a grudge. "

"So this Radel was the man in the green sedan" said Brady.

"Precisely."

Carmady's face was expressionless as he removed the pipe he had been smoking from his mouth. "Where exactly did Ullrich fit in to all this?"

"Well, Ullrich had been in trouble with the Nazis before coming over here, so that goes back a long way. We got chapter and verse on him from immigration. Final details came through this morning, I believe you, also, were sent a copy of that report?"

Brady nodded, "Yes we were."

"Fine. Well the upshot is, when their little spy group of Bund members told them about Ullrich and the movie they sent this Radel over to stop it and kill him.

Brady frowned. "Just a minute. Are you saying this Radel killed Ullrich as well?"

Curtis was phlegmatic. "I don't think there can be much doubt about that. It's why he came. I'm sure you will find he sent the threatening letter and you had a sighting of the green sedan near the scene, did you not? What more proof do you need?"

Brady frowned again. He wasn't quite sure how they'd found out about the green sedan, but he decided not to mention it. "Well, there's a few other things that don't quite fit that theory. For one, the slugs removed from Ullrich's body were .32 caliber...."

"Lieutenant," said Curtis patiently. "Radel was a professional killer. He'd have been unlikely to use the same gun twice and make it easy for you to link the two killings. The first was on the spur of the moment, the second was carefully planned."

"Possibly," said Brady looking unconvinced. "But all that's been recovered so far is a Walther P.38 which I've no doubt will match the bullet we found in Senna's car, but leaves us with only circumstantial evidence on Ullrich. And another thing, why did Radel bother to send the note if he was going to kill Ullrich anyway?"

Curtis looked off balance for just a moment.

"The principal object, Lieutenant, was to stop the movie, but I can tell you other people at the studio also received letters. Killing Ullrich, who they wanted anyway, showed they meant business."

Brady sat back in resignation.

Malone's eyes, however, had suddenly begun to gleam. Circumstantial or not, an obvious scenario was presenting itself. He exchanged glances with Carmady, both thinking along the same lines.

Carmady leaned forward pipe in hand and looked at Curtis. "So what you're giving us is the solution to two murders and with the perpetrator dead, the state saves the considerable expense of further investigation and trial."

"And," added Malone. "We get the credit."

Curtis guessed that's what Malone had really been after all along, and sensed that Carmady also realised what two good solved cases would be worth in terms of press coverage.

"That is how we hoped you'd see it, Captain. We don't really want a lot made of the Nazi angle. From papers recovered at the scene we'll have a few contacts to mop up. That can be done quietly."

"So how do you suggest we write all this up?" asked Malone.

"That's entirely up to you, Captain, just no Nazis and no FBI."

Malone's face was a picture of contentment, he even smiled at Frank.

Brady hadn't quite finished however. "Just a minute. What about the two Bundists killed the other evening in Griffith Park. Aren't they part of this?"

"I did read about the accident, Lieutenant. It seemed to me merely that. How did you know these men were Bundists?

"We have our sources too, Mr Curtis."

"Quite. So what exactly is the problem?"

"Since one of the men had a stab wound, we're quite certain a third party was involved, someone we've not been able to trace." Brady looked at Frank darkly.

"Lieutenant, we also have several sources within the Bundist ranks, as you might imagine. It is not inconceivable that one of them was involved. He merely proved smarter than his captors." Curtis smiled easily. "Wouldn't you agree?"

Brady was left chewing dirt and he knew it. "What do we charge the other two men from the raid with?"

Curtis thought for a minute. "There's always illegal entry to a Warner's property, Lieutenant. But I'm sure if you check with the County Police you may find these two were responsible for a break-in at the Martin Aircraft factory last week-end. That should be worth a couple of years in San Quentin."

Frank, Merv and Lou stood out in the hall waiting for the elevator. "I'm glad you warned us about Malone, Frank" grinned Curtis.

"He did run true to form. Just as well you didn't mention what my role actually was, he'd have burst a blood vessel."

"No need for any more of this to come out than absolutely necessary," said Curtis quietly. "Nor indeed for the police to know about Beaumont's involvement. That's the one thing that would have sensationalized the whole story and sent all the rats in the pack scurrying for cover."

The elevator doors slid open.

"How did you get on with Jack Warner this morning by the way?" asked Fisk.

"Well, the story you came up with about the Nazis blackmailing Beaumont on underage sex was a peach, otherwise Jack's reaction might have been unpredictable. As it was, he agreed the best course of action was quietly phasing Beaumont out."

"What about getting Ullrich's killer?"

"That went down rather well, especially when I told him since it was an FBI operation he could never mention it. I gave him all the gory details, and he loved it. He told me he had a personal letter from Hoover about the movie and he was going to send him a print for a private screening."

"Well, Frank, looks like time to say goodbye. I'm sorry about your partner, but at least you had the satisfaction of seeing justice done."

"Thanks a lot, fellas."

Fisk grinned. "By the way, Frank, you ever need a job, you know where to come looking."

It was nearing five by the time Frank retrieved the LaSalle and headed back into Hollywood. He had a date with Lois for seven-thirty, so he still had time to drop in past the office and pick up any last messages.

His mind went back over the day's events. Curtis had certainly tied the whole thing up in a very neat bundle and dropped it in the DA's lap. Malone had been grinning like Sylvester the cat.

There were times when cover-ups were done for all the wrong reasons, just occasionally they were done for the right ones.

Ellie had gone when he got back to the office, but the Ullrich file was on his desk. On top were several photocopies of clippings from two New York dailies, dated 1938, and a short, typed note from Ellie explaining the results of her research. Frank sat for a long time in the fading light after reading it.

Just for a while he'd fooled himself into believing this case was all over.

Now he knew it wasn't.

32

Later that evening Frank drove the LaSalle west on Sunset passing his now darkened office building on the corner of Ivar. Neon signs, traffic lights, movie theaters and billboards came and went. Frank didn't see any of them. Tonight he wasn't thinking about the FBI, green sedans, Warner Brothers or movie stars. Tonight he was thinking about Lois.

From the moment they had met she'd never been very far from his thoughts. Some of those thoughts were more than he'd ever permitted himself to think of any woman. A very dangerous precedent, he knew, and one that could destroy him unless he was very careful. Right now he was aware of how very close to the edge he was. This was something outside any previous experience.

At precisely seven-thirty Frank turned into the parking court outside the Escorial apartments on Laurel. His first visit here seemed somehow a very long time ago. Lois answered the door moments after his ring.

"How about that," she said. "A punctual man."

She wore a beige and blue patterned sleeveless silk dress cut just below the knee, and belted at the waist. The neck was styled in a long vee, that showed the firm swell of her breasts. Her high-heeled, ankle strapped shoes were gleaming navy snake-grained calf.

She looked absolutely stunning.

He smiled, kissed her lightly on the lips and tried to keep his voice level as he breathed in the scent he had now discovered was Shalimar. "Never let it be said I keep a lady waiting."

She threw a white fur wrap around her shoulders and picked the matching navy bag off the chair.

"Shall we go?" she said, holding out her arm.

They sat in a booth at the Beverley Hills Brown Derby on the corner of Wilshire and Rodeo. Reservations were not always easy to get, but having booked a number of times for Ullrich she knew who to talk to.

They talked of practically everything but the events of the last few weeks. As if somehow trying to find some common ground, other than that which they'd recently travelled. Each aware that what happened here might affect the whole future of their relationship. It was after midnight when he drove her home.

Lois went to the small bar, mixed two gimlets and passed one over to Frank, holding up the bottle of Rose's Lime Juice as she did so.

"Never fear," she laughed. "Only the real thing used here." She sat down opposite him on the davenport, knees together, with the glass in her hands. "Don't you think it's about time you told me what's really on your mind, Frank," she said softly. Her eyes were deep blue pools.

Frank put his drink down on the glass topped table beside a green jade ashtray and took out a cigarette.

"It would never work, would it, Lois?" He said taking a light. "You and I?"

She sat without moving, not drinking. "Why do you say that?"

"To start with we're from two different worlds."

"Different worlds?"

"You probably make quite a few bucks over there at Warners, Lois....... but not really enough to afford all this."

"All what?" she faltered.

"The dresses, Lois. You didn't really borrow them from the wardrobe department did you? The car, this apartment. You don't really share it with anyone else, do you?"

"No," she said in a small voice. "How did you know?"

"I'm a detective, Lois, that's what I do." His voice was a little offhand now. "According to my information you come from Richmond, Indiana, and your parents are, by any standard, very wealthy."

"That's not important," she said immediately, tossing her head.

"Oh but it is, Lois, it's very important. Because once you've lived like that you wouldn't want it any other way. You might give it up for a while, for fun, but very soon you'd want it all again, then the problems would really start."

She sat silently still not drinking, but staring into her glass, not wanting to look at him.

He went on. "When I left Homicide this afternoon everything seemed cut and dried, all the bases covered. The last piece in place. I had some small doubts, but they didn't seem important." He paused again. "But they're not really, are they, Lois?"

She looked back at him now, a little puzzled. "What do you mean?"

"When I got back to the office, late this afternoon, there was some information waiting for me. The final pieces in a very complex jigsaw. I told you we'd been checking into Ullrich's background to see if there was any other reason for the threatening letters."

"Yes, I recall." Her voice faltered slightly.

"Well, today I received some press clippings from the *New York Post* dated April 1938.... nothing earth-shattering about that really, except for the name.

"What name?" she said dully.

"Jean Paul."

"So?" Her eyes were dark, her face like stone.

"That was the name of a girl Ullrich was having an affair with in New York. She was in a play he was producing, that is until he fired her. The clipping was a report of her suicide."

"Why are you telling me this?" she cried. "I don't understand what this has got to do with me."

Frank paused again, aware of how cruel and hard this was going to be. But he had to go on.

"Jean Paul, however, was only a stage name," he said quietly. "Her real name was Paula...." The expression on her face told him that all pretence was gone. "The girl in the photograph on your nightstand, Lois. Your sister.... Paula Jean Cain."

She looked stricken.

"That is why you had to kill Ullrich, isn't it?" he went on softly.

Her expression suddenly changed to puzzlement and disbelief, then defiance. "That's an awful thing to say. How could you possibly come to that conclusion? You told me this morning the case was solved, a man named Radel was the killer." Her eyes burned. "Just because my sister was involved doesn't mean I killed him."

Frank drew calmly on his cigarette, he knew the pain this was causing. "No, that's perfectly true. And as far as the cops and the FBI are concerned the case is closed, so anything that happens here tonight is really rather academic. But it won't alter the facts for someone who has to live with them."

"You haven't answered the question." she said flatly.

Frank tapped some ash off his cigarette. "From the first moment I met you, Lois, I knew you weren't some farm girl from a hick town in Iowa. Yet there you were pretending to be a secretary. A producer's secretary maybe, but still a secretary. With looks like yours you could have been a star in no time at all. Perhaps there would have been a price to pay for that, but it's one most girls seem prepared to pay. No, Lois, from the outset everything about you screamed money. So the first question was, what were you really doing here?"

She looked directly at him, her face regaining some composure. "Okay, Frank, you want the truth. Here it is. I did come out here to get a job with some crazy idea about revenge. What sort of revenge I wasn't sure. Fortunately for me Jean had used a stage name, Ullrich never suspected a thing. Besides his ego was too big for that. That newspaper doesn't mention that Paula was six months pregnant... and just twenty years old. I tried to warn her before she went what it would be like, but she took no notice. I'd always been there to protect her in the past, but this time I wasn't. She fell for the old routine, sleep with me and I'll make you a star."

She paused for a moment her hand tightening on the glass, her face still pale, but her voice hardened as she went on. "But of course he didn't, she was just something to be used and cast aside. Then when she began to show he fired her. She phoned me for help, she was desperate. Told me not to breathe a word to mom and dad. I said I would come, but before I could get to her she'd.......she'd taken the overdose."

She was gripping the glass so hard he thought she'd break it. Tears rolled down her cheeks. "That's the kind of lousy heel Ullrich was, but that still doesn't mean I killed him."

Frank still hadn't touched his drink, but sat with the smoke from his cigarette rising lazily in the air, watching her. There were times when he hated himself and the job, but it didn't prevent him from doing what had to be done.

"That was the part I could only guess at, of course," he said finally. "But the other things that point to you are standard text for any cop. You had motive and opportunity. When you went that night to pick up the changes in the script, you saw your chance. Maybe you didn't intend to kill him, but when you saw the photograph on his desk you snapped. Nobody could blame you for that."

Lois stared at him through her tears. "Photograph? What photograph?" she said sharply. "I was only there for a few minutes, I didn't even go into the study. He'd obviously been drinking and tried to get me to have a drink. Said I'd be a certainty in the movies. There was a part coming up just made for me. He'd fix it. When he tried to put his arm round me I knew exactly where that was leading, so I grabbed the file and got out quick."

This wasn't going according to the script. She'd have

had to be Bette Davis to put something like this over. Frank tried one out of left field.

"Do you have a gun, Lois?"

"As a matter of fact I do," she said, looking up. "Would you like to see it?"

Her candid response took him by surprise. Before he could answer she rose, put down her drink, went through to the bedroom and rummaged about in the wardrobe. After a moment or two she returned and handed him a flat box wrapped in plain paper.

"There," she said, her face impassive. "That's exactly how it was when I bought it. The moment I got it home I knew I'd never be able to use it."

He opened it up. It was a nickel-plated Browning .32 automatic with a white bone grip. There was a box of ten cartridges, all intact. He checked the barrel. It had never been fired.

"Satisfied?" she said picking up her drink again.

"I guess I am," he said slowly, stubbing out his cigarette in the ashtray. "It's always a mistake to start thinking about a home run before you make the strike, but I had to know the truth, Lois. It leaves me with a problem though. If Radel didn't kill him and you didn't kill him, who did?"

"Why are you so sure this Radel didn't do it?"

"The missing photograph. It was the first thing I noticed, but at the time it just seemed curious. When I read the press cutting I knew it had to be your sister. What possible reason would Radel have for taking that.

It made no sense. Which is why I was afraid everything pointed to you."

"I'm sorry to disappoint you." she smiled wanly.

Frank looked back at her suddenly unable to read anything in those big blue eyes. After tonight, anything there was between them might have gone forever, that much he had to accept. But he was who he was and nothing could change that. The next move would have to be up to her.

"So it follows," he said, sipping his gimlet at last. "You didn't send the first two notes either?"

"No, but I must confess when I saw them I thought if someone else was after him I could take some measure of satisfaction from that. But whatever happened, I knew it would never bring my sister back."

Her face was still unreadable, but her eyes had begun to glisten again with tears. Frank stood up to go, and put his unfinished drink on the table. In that moment the final scene was unrolling behind his eyes, like a clip from a movie. He saw, with absolute clarity, how it must have gone down.

"Ullrich paid a heavy price for what he did and perhaps justice has been done. But there's still another roll of the dice to come."

"What do you mean?" she said.

"Whoever sent the notes must be the real killer."

33

The wipers on the La Salle were doing their best to keep up with the heavy rain that Monday morning as Frank drove out to the studio. No doubt it would clear by the afternoon, it usually did. Then the city would feel clean for a while.

All roads in Hollywood they say, lead to Warner Brothers. At least that's what Jack Warner would have everyone believe. Although he'd get a damn good argument from Sam Goldwyn and L.B. Mayer about that.

He and Lois had talked for a little longer last night, neither one wanting to admit things might never be quite the same again. She had even told him, in a moment of candour, that her date at Cyrano's had been with Beaumont. He, of course, mentioned nothing to her about Beaumont's part in the events. It remained to be seen whether the gap between them was unbridgeable. If so, then he couldn't complain. That's the way it was.

He'd spent a restless night going over events and wondering if anything he had done could have changed the outcome. He decided there wasn't, but a puzzle was never solved until the last piece was in place. That was what he was about to do now.

There was a new man on the gate in place of Owens whose only view at the moment, he suspected, was a barred window in a cell downtown. Frank showed his pass and was waved through. This would probably be the last time he'd use it. On the seat beside him was the final report for Jack Warner, but he had some other business to attend to first.

He drove around to the rear of the building, found a space and parked. The rain had eased a little, but still dripped off his hat. He checked the rows of cars and walked up and down until he found what he expected to find.

There was the usual hubbub on the third floor of the writers building and the notice on the door was still pinned up. He didn't knock. Two rather surprised faces looked up from their battered Remingtons as he entered.

"Kemo Sabay, here you are again," said Bert, whose quip was quickest off the mark. "I thought the case was solved and you'd ridden off into the setting sun."

A shadowy smile crossed Frank's face as took off his hat and shook off the rainwater. "I confess I'm just a little way off from shouting Hi-Yo, Silver."

Al and Bert grinned and raised their mugs of coffee in silent tribute.

"I always said he was sharp," said Al.

"Are you going to keep us in suspense or what?" rejoined Bert.

"Not much longer," replied Frank. "You know how irritating it can be when you can't find the last piece to a puzzle?"

"We certainly do," they chorused together.

"Well, I think I've finally found that last piece." The only sound was the rain gusting now and then against the window pane.

"Go on," said Bert.

"When I asked you earlier about the Ullrich affair in New York, you told most of the story....but not quite all."

"We......." started Al.

Frank pressed on.

"You both knew Ullrich was having an affair with that girl. You might even have suspected she was pregnant, which she was. She may not have been very good, and Ullrich would probably have kept her on but for that."

Both writers had lost their look of bonhomie.

"Shall I go on?" queried Frank.

Bert nodded without comment.

"But one thing neither of you knew........ Jean Paul's real name."

They both shook their heads lamely.

"Paula Jean Cain........ Lois's sister."

There was stunned silence in the room.

"Lois?" said Al in a strangled voice.

"Unbelievable," said Bert. "Why would she come and work for Ullrich of all people?" The answer seemed to come to him before the question was out of his mouth. "You think maybe she came here to get some sort of revenge? To kill him maybe?"

"That's precisely why she came. Of course she didn't know anything about the two of you, or your involvement with Ullrich in New York. Never even suspected it. Not until I came on the scene anyway."

Bert pushed back his chair.

"But she couldn't have. According to the morning paper a suspect was shot dead in a police raid last Friday." said Al.

"Ah well, but we all know that isn't true," said Frank with a cool smile. "Don't we?"

"This is totally bewildering," said Bert. "Are you saying then that Lois did kill him?"

"Funnily enough, until last night I thought she had, but I have to admit I got it wrong."

"Then who the hell did do it?" cried Bert.

"Whichever one of you owns that green Dodge out there in the car park." Frank said matter-of-factly, looking at each of them in turn.

It seemed, for a moment, as if the whole building had gone silent. Al half stood, then sat down again, his face turning an ashen grey.

"It......it's mine," he said simply.

Bert was aghast. He looked across the desk. "Al, I don't believe it. You killed Ullrich! Why for God's sake? I know we did those joke letters together, but I never really thought you were serious."

Frank waited for Al to answer.

"Bert...Bert, you can't imagine the pain. I......I was in love with Jean. I know she liked me and, but for that swine Ullrich she might have loved me. But he was always making her promises, which he never intended to keep, just so he could get her into bed."

He paused and put his hands up to his face. Then he continued. "I asked her out once, but she said she had to read a script for Ullrich. After she left I tried to find her, but couldn't find out where she lived. There was a rumour she was pregnant, but we didn't find out for certain until later. By that time Ullrich had left for Hollywood. When we got the job here I knew it was my opportunity and I was determined to get some sort of revenge. I just had to wait for the right moment." He looked at Frank kind of blankly. "How did you find out?"

"The photograph Al, the photograph. You took it didn't you?"

Al nodded silently.

"I don't understand," said Bert looking at Frank.

"I spoke to Brady this morning, and asked him why he voiced doubt over Radel as the killer. Since the case was offically closed, he didn't mind telling me. An empty frame on Ullrich's desk was wiped clean of prints, he said, and that could only mean one thing. The killer must have removed the picture. Since Ullrich's name was never linked with the suicide, police enquiries in New York came up clean. So they were forced to think the photo was something to do with Ullrich's Austrian past. With me so far?"

"I think so," said Bert. "Go on."

Frank looked at Al. "But of course it was nothing of the sort. It was a picture of Paula. Why he kept it, we'll never know. Perhaps it reminded him of his conquest. The photo presented you with a dilemma, Al. Had you left it, there was always the slim chance someone might make the connection, depending on what came out of the case. Besides the thought of her picture on Ullrich's desk was more than you could stand, wasn't it?"

Al's face was pale but composed. He spoke quietly. "It would be true to say that picture got Ullrich killed."

"Hold on a minute, Frank," said Bert, "we seem to have leapt ahead here. How did you know about the car?"

"Well, I'll cut a long story short," said Frank. "Our Nazi killer had been tailing me around town for the last three weeks in a rented green Plymouth. He even tried a hit-and-run, that is quite apart from having two of his pals try to take me on a one-way trip to Griffth Park."

"My God, why was he doing that?"

"Because..... Because he thought I knew who he was

and why he was here." That wasn't all the story but it was as much as he was going to tell them.

"Go on," said Bert.

"The police had a witness who saw a green sedan, near Ullrich's on the night of the killing, but it wasn't a positive I.D. so they didn't know the make. When later they found Radel had been driving a green sedan, they assumed it was him."

"So how did you connect that with Al?"

"By working backwards. When I made the connection between Paula and Lois, I leapt to the conclusion that Lois had killed Ullrich. All the things that applied to Al also applied to her. She also would have removed the photograph, and of course she had freely admitted to being the last person to see Ullrich alive. Barring the actual killer that is. Does that make sense?"

"Yes, yes, I think so. But if you thought Lois had killed him, how could you have explained the car?"

"Well, that wasn't too difficult. We knew Radel was here to kill Ullrich. He could easily have come that night with the intention, but arrived too late. The deed as they say, had already been done."

"Circumstantially that's okay," said Bert. "But he would have denied it, surely?"

"No doubt, Bert, but he was dead before anyone could ask him. In turn, however, if Lois *hadn't* killed him, then whoever was driving that green sedan became the prime suspect."

"Which brings us back to the photograph, and why it couldn't have been Radel. Right?"

"Right," said Frank. "There's one thing that does bother me, Al. Why did you wait so long after sending the notes to take any action?"

Al pulled himself up from the slumped position in his chair. "When Bert and I sent the notes it was really just a game to frighten him, make the bastard feel a little of what Jean must have felt. But if they had any effect on him it didn't show. We were just wondering what to do next when you showed up. Of course, we didn't know if it was in response to the notes or the accidents on the set."

He paused, a thin line of perspiration shone on his upper lip. He looked at Frank and went on.

"Then I found out Ullrich really did have another writing team ready to take over after we finished this picture. He was just using us the way he used everybody. So, with nothing to lose and without telling Bert, I decided to give him the fright of his life. Make him face death like Jean must have faced it. So you see I never really intended to kill him.....things just went...well... wrong, I can't prove that of course, but it's the truth." His voice trailed away, he was staring straight ahead like someone in a dream.

"I chose a Sunday night," Al continued, his voice mechanical, "when I knew he'd be home. It had been easy to get his address from the files. I parked some way from the house, ducked into the trees and walked down unseen. When I got there I was horrified to see Lois going in. I hung around for a few minutes trying to decide what to do, then next thing she was leaving."

"Go on," said Frank.

"I found him in the study at the back. The French door was open. He looked up in astonishment when I walked in and asked what the fuck I was doing there. The first thing I saw was the picture of Jean on his desk, for some reason he'd been looking at it. Then he saw me looking at it too. He sat back grinning, so that's what this is about, he said. I said yes. Then took out the gun and told him I was going to kill him for what he did to her. I really wanted to make him think I would."

Al stopped for a moment, staring into space. Then continued in the same mechanical voice.

"He called me a bloody fool. She wasn't interested in you he said, she wanted to be a star. Maybe, I said. But you took that away from her. His face began to show fear for the first time. I aimed the gun over his head and pulled the trigger, but nothing happened. As I fumbled with the safety, he stood up and said 'Lois....' then suddenly the gun went off, and hit him in the chest. It must have killed him straightaway, because he didn't say any more, he just flopped down..."

Al's voice faltered. "You....you know the rest, I took the photograph out, remembered to wipe the frame and ran, I knew no-one would believe it was an accident."

"No I'm sure they wouldn't," mused Frank. "One

thing though, any idea why he mentioned Lois?"

"None at all."

"You said he had Paula's picture out front?"

"Yes I did."

"Maybe he'd made the connection between them and was trying to tell you."

Al's face was without expression. "Well it's over now and I can't say I'm sorry."

Bert looked across at his friend, then anxiously at Frank.

"What happens now?"

Frank was solemn. "Nothing as far as I know."

"Nothing?"

"Not a goddamn thing. The cops are happy, most of them anyway. The FBI are happy, they've got their killer. This case is all wrapped up in a nice neat bundle with a large bow. If you went downtown and confessed to an accident, when they've solved a nice juicy murder, they'd throw you out the door."

"But....but people will know, won't they?"

"Well I won't tell anyone if you don't, and since we're the only ones who know, there isn't much chance of that. In a weird sort of way justice has been done."

Al tried a pale smile. "I'm sort of glad I've been able to tell someone. It's a been rather a strain."

"Well, don't worry too much. They just dug one of my slugs out of Radel."

"You were there?" said Bert incredulously.

"I was. Three weeks ago that bastard killed my

partner, just because he was in the wrong place at the wrong time." He held up his hand. "That's all I can tell you, so don't ask for an explanation. You will, of course, be able to read all about it in the newspaper. It won't be the truth, and it won't mention me, but it's near as you're going to get.

So now you know something neither of you can talk about. Now, gentlemen, if you don't mind, I've an appointment with a certain Mr Jack Warner."

34

Harry's Bar on Sunset was crowded with regulars. The juke box was playing a Tommy Dorsey number "Smoke Gets in Your Eyes," and everything in the world seemed hunky-dory.

It just goes to show how wrong you can be.

The case was solved and everybody had got what they wanted. So although they all thought they knew what had happened, they didn't. They just knew their particular version. Frank knew most of it but he wasn't telling anybody. Those were his own rules, so he couldn't blame anyone else for that.

He sat at the far end of the long black bar, a double vodka gimlet in front of him. Lois hadn't been in the office when he'd dropped in for a last goodbye, Al and Bert however had promised to keep in touch.

There were a couple of new cases lying on his desk and he hadn't paid any bills for a fortnight. Mind you that didn't worry him too much when he thought about the check he'd got from Jack Warner. Still it was hard to believe it was all over. He felt a vague sense of restlessness unlike anything he'd known before.

He glanced absently at the newspaper lying on the bar. It had been a slow time for news until this case had come along. Not all the story was out yet of course, just the shoot-out at Alta Brea. There was a big spread on that, including pictures of Malone and the D.A. Details of the connection with the Ullrich and Senna murders would come later, the result of brilliant police work no doubt. If there was one thing the department was good at it was the manipulation of a story.

The studio, on the other hand, would turn its very able publicity machine to work and the public would flock to see Ullrich's last movie. There was one consolation, however: Beaumont would find himself making B-movies in remote parts of the country for some considerable time to come.

All that paled into insignificance when he thought about Lois. It seemed to him they should make all women like her or none at all. It was just too damn painful when you fell for them. Just a week ago he felt he had the world at his feet, now it was on his back. He gazed at the remnants of the gimlet in his glass and signalled the bartender. Life would go on, a new adventure would start tomorrow, it always had.

He glanced around. The hum of conversation had died down suddenly and the noise of traffic on the boulevard was apparent through the open door.

Lois was standing just inside the entrance, eyes adjusting to the sudden gloom. She wore a dark blue flared polka dot dress, which looked like it cost more than he earned in a week, with a white jacket and strapped shoes. Her hair was caught back in a pony tail and around her neck was a matching scarf. She was pulling off her white kid gloves when she spotted him.

That walk the length of the bar was worth a million dollars to see. Had Jack Warner been there he would have signed her on the spot. Certainly Harry's bar would never see anything like it again.

She paused by the red leather stool next to him. "This seat taken?" she asked.

"Not so far as I'm aware," he responded cautiously.

Just then the bartender returned with Frank's vodka gimlet.

"Don't I get one?" she murmured sliding on to the stool.

"Coming up, lady," said the bartender smoothly before Frank could answer. She slipped her gloves under the strap of her alligator bag and put it down beside her.

"How did you find me?" he managed to say.

"I asked around."

"Oh," he said.

She looked back at him with those big blue eyes.

There was a certain luminosity in them he somehow hadn't noticed before. It seemed to him he was always discovering something new about her. Her face had that infinite capacity for change.

"I spoke to Bert and Al," she said, looking directly at him. "They told me what you did."

"Just preserving the status quo," said Frank, looking into his drink. "I figured we could all use a little help coming to terms with what happened."

He knew he was going to need a lot of help coming to terms with what was sitting next to him. The barman put a napkin carefully on the black counter, placed her drink on it, then reluctantly moved away.

"I suppose you're wondering why I'm here?" she said tasting her drink.

"The thought was in the process of crossing my mind."

"Well, maybe I can help it on its way a little. I spoke with my father on the telephone this morning and told him I had decided to come home for a while. But I have a few hours before I leave. I saw no reason why I should spend them alone."

"I see. Had you anything particular in mind?"

She gazed at him levelly in that straightforward way she had. "We could go to my apartment and make love if you like."

Frank's glass was halfway to his mouth. He put it down again. "What time is your train?" was all he could reply.

ROBERT HAYDEN

"Not until ten. I musn't miss it though or Daddy will be upset."

"We'd better get a move on then, we certainly don't want to upset Daddy."